GUNSMOKE
AND
TRAIL DUST

Center Point
Large Print

Also by Bliss Lomax and available from
Center Point Large Print:

The Phantom Corral

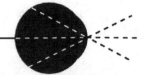

**This Large Print Book carries the
Seal of Approval of N.A.V.H.**

GUNSMOKE
AND
TRAIL DUST

Bliss Lomax

CENTER POINT LARGE PRINT
THORNDIKE, MAINE

First US Edition: Dodd, Mead and Company, Inc.
First UK edition: Wells Gardner

The text of this Large Print edition is unabridged.
In other aspects, this book may vary
from the original edition.
Printed in the United States of America
on permanent paper.
Set in 16-point Times New Roman type.

ISBN: 978-1-68324-592-6 (hardcover)
ISBN: 978-1-68324-596-4 (paperback)

Library of Congress Cataloging-in-Publication Data

Names: Lomax, Bliss, 1888–1979, author.
Title: Gunsmoke and trail dust / Bliss Lomax.
Description: Center Point large print edition. | Thorndike, Maine :
    Center Point Large Print, 2017.
Identifiers: LCCN 2017039222| ISBN 9781683245926
    (hardcover : alk. paper) | ISBN 9781683245964 (pbk. : alk. paper)
Subjects: LCSH: Large type books. | GSAFD: Western stories.
Classification: LCC PS3507.R1745 G86 2017 | DDC 813/.54—dc23
LC record available at https://lccn.loc.gov/2017039222

List of Chapters—

Chapter One

Trouble!

Harvey Hume rode into Mescal this morning without any premonition of impending trouble. He was barely twenty-one, but he had been doing a man's work for five years, and it had rubbed all the boyishness out of his young face. He had a keen sense of perception, and as he jogged up the street, he was quick to sense the uneasy quiet and air of suppressed excitement that had descended on the town.

For a Friday morning, Mescal was crowded. A score of horses stood at the hitchracks. They bore familiar brands. Harvey had only to run his eye over them to know who was in town. It was enough to tighten his mouth unconsciously, and he jogged on with a definite sense of anxiety stealing over him.

A little group of men, Mormon homesteaders like himself, had gathered in front of Downie's blacksmith shop to listen to tall, bearded Webb Nichols, regarded by many as their potential leader if the long conflict with the big cow outfits flamed into violence again.

"What's this all about, Webb?" Harvey

inquired, as he stepped down from the saddle.

"The Association is havin' a special meetin'," Nichols answered soberly. "Ringe can't usually git enough of 'em together for a quorum, but they're all up there this mornin'—the whole sixteen of 'em!" With a jerk of his head he indicated the lodge room above the firehouse across the way. "Reckon there's no question about what it means!"

The others nodded grimly. One said, "They're fixin' to do somethin' about the rustlin'. If John Ringe has his way, they'll bring in a bunch of gun slingers, same as they did seven years ago!"

"If they do, rustling will be only the excuse; the real purpose will be to make trouble for us!" another declared bitterly.

"It's a little late for us to be complaining," Harvey said coolly. "If the Association turns loose a bunch of gunmen, we can blame ourselves. We've been asking for it for a long time. Trying to get even wasn't the way to end this trouble."

"Harvey, yo're a fool, sayin' anythin' like that!" Nichols whipped out angrily. "What would you have had us do—turn the other cheek to those range hogs after what they done to us? They killed yore pa when they tried to run us out, seven years ago. Are you forgittin' that?"

"No, I'm not forgetting it." Harvey realized

they were all against him. He had the courage of his convictions, however, and he faced them defiantly. "But always preaching hatred and trying to keep the old grudges alive will never bring peace to the basin. You know as well as I do that we're responsible for most of this rustling. We've got the votes today; we can pack a jury and acquit a man, no matter how much evidence there is against him. We've done it time after time."

"It's no more'n Ringe and his friends had comin' to 'em!" Webb protested vehemently. "If they want to make somethin' of it, let 'em!"

It was what the others wanted to hear. The youngster could only regard them pityingly, knowing it was useless to say anything further. Years of conflict had so embittered them that when trouble threatened, their only recourse was to rally around men like Webb Nichols. But there were other young men like himself who felt as he did.

"When you start whooping up the war talk, you want to remember you're speaking for yourselves this time," he told them. "There's some of us who don't propose to be dragged into another fight."

Turning to his bronc, he swung up and jogged off on the business that had brought him to town.

Mescal was the same sun-bleached Arizona

cow town he had first seen as a boy of fourteen. Cut off to the south from the rest of the state by the mighty gorge of the Colorado, and still as far as ever from a railroad, its only contact with the outside world was through southern Utah.

And yet, in ways that didn't meet the eye, Mescal had changed. The town was no longer subject to the dictates of the dozen or more Magdalena Basin stockmen who once had had undisputed sway over this wide stretch of country from the Grand Wash to Hurricane Ledge. Out in the basin, the changes were more apparent. Harvey Hume could remember it when it was unbroken free-range. It was dotted with small ranches like his own today.

Harvey left his bronc at the hitchrack in front of the post office and stepped inside. Dad Beazley, the postmaster, was behind the counter.

"Did yuh see any signs of the meetin' breakin' up as you came up the street?" Dad inquired, running through the mail in the H pigeonhole.

"No, they're still up there, Dad."

The old man found several letters and the weekly paper from St. George for him.

"Reckon that's all there is, Harvey." He pushed the mail across the counter. He looked up suddenly, his eyes bright and keen in his shrewd, puckish face. He liked to pop a question at a man and catch him by surprise. "What yuh figger they're plannin' to do?"

"I don't know. Put down the rustling, I suppose."

Ab Beazley shook his head pessimistically. "That's easier said than done, mister! This corner of Arizona has allus been a rustler's paradise. If a man's got to make a run for it, he can head west and be in Nevada in a few hours. Don't take even that long to git acrost the Utah line."

A faded reward notice was posted on the wall. Five hundred was offered for information leading to the arrest and conviction of one Steve Jennings, a known rustler. Dad indicated the notice with a jerk of his head.

"That thing's been up there a year. Offerin' rewards and dependin' on the law to trip him won't bother Steve none."

"Nor any of the rest of them, Dad. They've got the run of all that wild, mountain country east of the basin. Nobody's going to go looking for them up on those timbered plateaus."

"I dunno!" Dad contradicted thoughtfully. "There's men with guts enough to go after 'em and hang on to their trail all the way down through the red bluffs to the Colorado, if need be. We did it more'n once when I was a young man. We carried the law with us on our saddles, and when we caught our rustlers, we strung 'em up where we found 'em, and no nonsense about bringin' 'em into Mescal to have a jury say whether they was guilty or not. That's the way to handle things! Stretch a few necks and it'll drive a wedge between these cow thieves and you folks in the basin and bring some of yuh to yore senses!"

Harvey was used to old Ab's violent harangues and positive opinions. "I thought you were neutral, Dad," he said, lightly.

"And so I am!" the postmaster insisted fiercely. "I allus claimed no one side had all the right with 'em. But I draw the line at protectin' blacklegs, Harvey! The Association don't want another war any more'n you little fellers, and when they got together this mornin', I figgered it wouldn't take 'em ten minutes to decide that the only way to clear the air was to fergit all about the law and hang every rustler they got their hands on. But they bin up there waggin' their tongues fer over an hour." Ab shook his head disgustedly. "Seems like the dang fools don't know how to pull together no more!"

That was stating the case correctly, for the special meeting of the Magdalena Stockmen's Association had produced some wide differences of opinion among its members. A proposition had been placed before the organization. Hot words and pointed accusations had been tossed back and forth across the long table, in the lodge room over the firehouse, and most of them had been directed at John Ringe, its author.

But storms were of no consequence to him,

and it was not until the course he had counseled appeared to be getting lost in acrimonious debate that he got to his feet and rapped for attention. He was a big man, as straight and sturdy as he stood there as one of the giant yellow pines that dotted his Santa Bonita ranch. His hair, long, flowing mustache, and bushy brows were as white as the snow that tipped those pines in winter.

"It won't do us any good to sit here wrangling all day," he said, with unexpected patience. "We're all agreed that something will have to be done. If you won't go along with what I proposed, suggest something of your own, but don't tell me there's any sense in waiting for the law to step in and put down this rustling. We pay the taxes and foot the bill for this end of the country, but we don't have any more to say about how things are run than a bunch of Piute Indians!"

"Damn my britches if that ain't the truth!" a fiery little man at the end of the table burst out, as big John sat down. He banged the table with his fist to give emphasis to his feelings. His face was the color of old saddle leather, and wind and sun had dried him out so thoroughly there wasn't much left of him but skin and bones. With his hooked nose and faded, squinting eyes of the desert man, he looked like nothing so much as a scrawny old eagle.

In the dim past he had answered to the name of Robert, but northern Arizona knew him as Coconino Williams, the first white man to run cattle in Magdalena Basin. He glared around the room, challenging anyone to take issue with him.

"Most of these damned nesters wouldn't know where their next meal was comin' from if they couldn't go out and drop their loop on our beef! But they kin vote, and that's all that bunch of political tinhorns down in Kingman is interested in! A tax collector and a deputy sheriff who wouldn't make an arrest if you rubbed a cow thief under his nose is the size of what we git fer our money!"

His inflammatory words received the hearty approval of some. Ed Stack, an unsmiling man, who sat at Coconino's elbow was unmoved by it. Of all the men seated at the table, only John Ringe ranged more cattle than he.

"We all know what the situation is," he said in his determined, unhurried way. "What we're looking for is something that will improve it." He wasn't speaking for himself alone. All through the meeting he had had the support of the faction that hoped to avoid hostilities. "Mebbe we'd do better if we tried to get along with these homesteaders instead of always bucking them tooth and nail. We made a mistake seven years ago, and we've been paying for it ever since. I let you and John talk me into that,

14

Coconino. I'm telling you flatly I won't be a party to bringing in gunmen a second time."

John Ringe reared up, shaking his head like an angry mountain lion, his patience a thing of the past.

"You can't twist my proposition into anything like that!" he roared. "I'm not asking this Association to bring in gunmen! I'm asking for a first-rate stock-detective—a man who can throw the fear of God into these rustlers and stop 'em! When you throw it up to me that we made a mistake seven years ago, I can tell you the only mistake we made was in not going through with what we started! We weren't dealing with homesteaders then; Virgil and Travis Hume were the only ones who had title to the land they occupied; the rest were just squatters! They'd have gone, and there wouldn't have been any bloodshed if Virgil Hume hadn't fired the first shot!"

"Times have changed, John," Pat Redman, Ringe's neighbor on the Santa Bonita, spoke up. He had lost a son in what was always referred to as the Magdalena Basin War. "The less that's said about the past, the better. I agree with Stack that these folks is here to stay. That don't mean we've got to stand for the deal they're handin' us. I wouldn't be up on my ear if it was just a case of them helpin' themselves to a little of my beef now and then. But damn their hides, they're coverin' up for the real rustlers! I don't know how the rest of you figger it, but I reckon if we put our losses together we'd find that seven, eight hundred head of cattle was hazed up Cochinilla Wash and through the Desolation Mountains this past year."

"I reckon it'd be nearer a thousand head!" old Coconino interjected shrilly. "And once they got 'em across the Utah line into that San Juan country, we kin kiss 'em good-by! The stuff is sold to that rustlin' ring up there and sent on to Wyomin'! You know that as well as I do! If we're goin' to stop it, we got to stop it here! Clay Roberts is the man fer the job. If he'll take it, I say, send fer him!"

"So do I!" Redman seconded heartily. "If he can do half as good for us as he's done for stock associations in West Texas and New Mexico, I say send for him, John, and to hell with hagglin' over what it costs! He's a lone wolfer, and he gets results. I've heard tell of how he went down into the Pecos River country and cleaned it out singlehanded. When he moves in, rustlers move out! And by damnation, that's what we want!"

It was greeted with varying degrees of approval by some. Ed Stack and his following signified their opposition. John Ringe glanced about the room, counting noses. His hasty tabulation warned him that sentiment was about evenly divided. Bristling with indignation, he focused his attention on Stack.

"Ed, you admit we've got to do something. Why are you opposed to hiring Roberts?"

"Clay Roberts is a killer," Stack declared soberly. "Turn him loose and we'll have a war on our hands whether we want it or not. I know his record. He gets results, but he gets them with his trigger finger."

"Wal, I'm everlastin'ly bedamned, if that don't take the cake!" Coconino Williams howled. "You aimin' to hire a hoss doctor for this job, Ed? I don't care how many rustlers Roberts kills!"

"Nor I!" Stack flared back hotly. "But this ain't a two-sided fight. It won't be only rustlers he'll go after; he'll make a mistake and some homesteader will get knocked off. The fat will be in the fire, then."

"That's nonsense!" Big John boomed. "Clay Roberts didn't make his reputation by bungling things that way! When I was in Denver last fall, I spoke to a dozen men who know him—U.S. marshals, stockmen, and the manager of the Pinkerton office—and they all have the highest regard for him. When I first wrote Roberts, I told him exactly what the situation was. I explained that we didn't want any trouble with these folks in the basin. He told me he knew of no reason why there should be trouble with them. And he guaranteed me if there was, it wouldn't be of his making. I'm chairman, so I don't feel free to make a motion—"

"I'll make it!" Coconino called out. "I move that—"

"Just a minute!" Ringe interjected. "The majority may feel that the Association shouldn't take any action. If that's the way it turns out, I won't be a dog in the manger. On the other hand, if we're going to do anything, we want to do it today. It'll take Roberts a week to get here. The snow is going off up in the mountains. The passes will be open before we're half done with the spring work. The next we'll hear is that someone is losing stock. Charlie Petrie was the first one to holler last year. Are you going to stand by and let them get in on you again this spring, Charlie?"

The question sounded innocent enough, but the big man from the Santa Bonita wasn't as guileless as he pretended, for Petrie had stood with Stack all through the meeting. Now that the spotlight was turned on him, he squirmed in his chair.

"By grab, I'm goin' to stop 'em if I can," Petrie declared uneasily. "I know I can't stand another dose like last year. There ought to be somethin' we could do." He glanced at Stack, as he wavered in his allegiance. "If Roberts will do as he says, mebbe we ought to hire him, Ed."

It broke the back of the opposition. Another man switched sides. It left no doubt of the outcome. When the vote was taken, Stack stood alone.

"Why don't you change yore vote and make it unanimous, Ed?" Coconino urged. Stack shook his head.

"That ain't necessary. Things have gone your way, and I'll have to go along with you. I only hope it doesn't turn out to be a mistake."

Ringe penned a letter to Roberts, and when it had been approved, the meeting broke up. Down the street, at the post office, the northbound stage for St. George and the railroad, at Lund, Utah, was waiting. When it pulled out in its long, 100-mile journey, the summons from the Association was in the mail pouch.

Chapter Two

Old Grudges

News of the action the Association had taken ran from lip to lip and was all over town before the stage was out of sight. Frank Dufors, the deputy sheriff, was among the first to hear it. He made his permanent headquarters in Mescal and was the sole representative of the law in that part of the county. Dufors, a rangy Texan, with an unpleasantly prominent jaw, was well aware of the contempt in which he was held by the big cowmen. It bothered him not at all, for he was cunning enough to realize that it wasn't men like John Ringe and Stack and old Coconino Williams who buttered his bread. He had played his cards carefully in the three years he had served under Sheriff Hector Barry, who appeared in Mescal only at six-month intervals.

In miles, the county seat was not so far away. But to reach Mescal, Barry had to cross over into Nevada, take the railroad to Lund and come down by stage. This isolation gave Dufors such authority as a deputy sheriff seldom enjoyed.

Even so, Frank Dufors was a dissatisfied, embittered man, for though he nursed every dollar out of his job that he could find ways of extracting, the pay was poor. This morning, as he sat in his little adobe brick jail, moodily contemplating the step the Association had taken, he was overwhelmed by the sorry realization that he was a big frog in a very small pond.

Old jealousies and enmities boiled up in Dufors, for Clay Roberts was no stranger to him. In the long ago, they had started out on even terms in the Texas Panhandle. He damned the whim of fate that seemed to have gone out of its way to throw them together again.

Webb Nichols, who had called young Harvey Hume a fool, walked in as Dufors sat slouched down at his table. "Reckon you've heard what they done," he said.

"Yeh," Dufors growled. "How do you boys feel about it?"

"Wal, we expected worse," Webb declared frankly. "We shore figgered they was goin' to turn a bunch of gun slingers loose. Don't seem like one man could make much hell for us, though I reckon he'll have his nose into everythin'."

"He won't push you folks around if I know it!" Dufors said flatly. "Roberts has got a big reputation, but he's just a stock-detective. He doesn't have any authority from the law. You men want to remember that. You don't have to get out of his way!"

Nichols eyed him shrewdly. "You sound as though you knew somethin' about him, Frank."

"I know all about him!" Dufors rapped. "He may be poison to some people, but he doesn't want to try to walk over me!"

His truculent manner and brave words failed to arouse any marked enthusiasm in Webb. The deputy sheriff had proved to be a pliant tool of the faction the bearded Mormon represented. It did not make for respect. In fact, Webb had a secret scorn for the man's judgment and courage. In the present instance, he felt that Dufors was only whistling in the dark in proclaiming what he was going to do, with Roberts still some hundreds of miles away.

"He's tough, eh?" he demanded bluntly, and there was a definite feeling of contempt in his eyes as he regarded Dufors.

"Sure, he's tough!" the latter growled. "I can be tough too! I don't propose to walk wide of him, I can tell you!"

Webb was not interested in Dufors' bragging; he wanted some information about the Association's new agent. With some prodding, he got it, and though he discounted some of it as exaggerated and biased, it was still of a nature to cause his habitual soberness to rest more heavily than usual on him as he turned down the street.

The group of men in front of the blacksmith shop had grown to a dozen or more. They gathered round Webb to hear what he had learned from Dufors. His news had a disquieting effect on all save Shad Caney, a dark-browed, violent-tempered man.

"Why the long faces?" Caney demanded fiercely. He was the only Gentile in the crowd. "I don't know what's got into you Mormons! There used to be some fight in you, but now you take back talk from a boy and pull in yore horns 'cause Ringe's crowd is bringin' in a stock-detective!"

"I ain't pullin' in my horns, nor am I figgerin' on goin' hog wild!" Webb said thinly, taking it as a personal affront. "You'll find me standin' up for my rights, no matter what they do!"

His dark eyes had narrowed with cold hostility. Caney and he had come in with the first settlers, but though they had gone through the Magdalena Basin War together, there was a long and bitter hatred between them that had flamed into gunfire on one occasion. A borrowed saddle, which Webb insisted Caney had never returned, was the cause of their long quarrel. Both were frugal and industrious and few among the basin homesteaders were as prosperous. Within the year they had been elected to the board of commissioners for the Willow Creek school, along with John Ringe. They were in Mescal today to attend a monthly meeting of the board.

"Lettin' a young squirt like Harvey Hume talk you down, and runnin' to Frank Dufors to see what he's goin' to do may be yore idea of standin' up for yore rights, but it ain't mine!" Shad snarled, ready, as usual, to make the most of anything from Webb that even faintly resembled a challenge. "If we play it yore way, them highbinders will have our ears pinned back before we do anythin'!"

Webb's rocky face drained white with wrath and he broke away from one of his adherents who tried to hold him back as he started to rush at Caney. Virgil Hume, Harvey's uncle, a brawny, barrel-chested man, famous all over the basin for his feats of strength, stepped in between them as they stood toe to toe, glaring their implacable hatred.

"Take it easy!" Virgil warned, getting them apart. "Shad, you got no call to be poppin' off. If trouble comes, we'll hold up our end, but as Webb says, we ain't goin' to be stampeded into doin' anythin' foolish."

He not only had the backing of the crowd but was formidable enough in his own right to be an effective, if unappreciated, peacemaker. Caney looked him over from head to toe.

"I know what you'll do!" he snorted contemptuously. "You'll steal off to meetin's like a bunch of scared rabbits till it's too late to do anythin' else!" He shoved through the crowd, growling, "I ain't interested in hearin' any more of yore mouthwash! You go yore way and I'll go mine!"

"Let him go," someone exclaimed. "He'll cool off."

"I don't care whether he does or not," said Virgil. "We've worked and fought too hard for what we've got to risk losin' everythin' by flyin' off half-cocked, as he'd have us do. If we have to start packin' our rifles, we'll do it; but no hothead is goin' to drag us into this fight if I have anythin' to say about it."

Webb Nichols and he were the best of friends, but the glance he gave the latter left no doubt that what he had said was as much for him as for anyone else.

Webb held his tongue. Though no one else seemed to notice, he caught a strong echo of the stand young Harvey was taking in what his uncle had to say.

It was almost noon, and in a few minutes the crowd began to melt away. Together, Webb and Hume walked down to the wagon yard of Huntsinger's livery stable to feed their teams. When the chore was finished they got their lunches from the wagons and sat down in the shade of the barn to eat.

"You haven't said anythin' in ten minutes, Webb," Virgil remarked. "I didn't hurt yore feelin's by anythin' I said, I hope."

"No, I was jest thinkin'. When Harvey pitched into me this mornin' I didn't know what to make of it. But I can see you feel about the same as he does. I never figgered he was gittin' such ideas from you."

Virgil shook his head. "It's the other way around; I been listenin' to him and the young fellows of his age. They were just boys when they came here. They've had a tough time, Webb; workin' themselves to the bone, and often never half enough to eat, while they was growin' up. Things are a little better now, and they want to hang on to what they got. They're willin' to forgit the old grudges. They claim Ed Stack and a couple others are ready to meet them halfway. I don't know; maybe they're all wrong. But they're young; maybe they've got more sense than we have."

"I doubt it!" Webb growled. "Their meddlin' won't help us none. It's too late, after all these years, to think anythin' can be worked out on those lines. You ought to be the one to know it."

"I suppose I should," Virgil admitted. "Ringe still says I fired the first shot, seven years ago. I've never let an opportunity slip to hurt 'em. I helped to acquit Mescalero Joe Salazar last fall when I knew he was guilty as a man ever

26

was. I wouldn't do it again—nor any of the other things. Like blowin' up Pat Redman's dam. I can see now that it was all wrong; peace could never come of it. Maybe Harvey and the other young fellows like him won't git very far with the stand they're takin' but they're entitled to a chance."

Webb Nichols stared at him, astounded. "I can't believe it!" he groaned. "You saw yore brother Travis killed, our homes burned down and our stock slaughtered by Ringe and the rest of 'em, and you can still talk of forgivin' those men and meetin' 'em halfway?"

Virgil nodded soberly. "More bloodshed won't bring Travis back. There's just a chance that Harvey may be right, and I'm stringin' along with him."

Chapter Three

The New Teacher

In the little white house wedged in between Stoddard's Drugstore and the Mescal Mercantile Company's establishment Eudora Stoddard hummed a gay little tune as she set the table for the noonday dinner. She wore her auburn hair pulled back rather tightly from her forehead and done up high in back, in the style of the day back East, from which she had come a few months ago. It made her look older than she was and gave her sensitive young face added dignity.

A tarnished spoon at her uncle's place caught her eye. She picked it up and examined it critically. "Egg stains!" she said to herself. "I better get it out of sight before Aunt Jude sees it."

She hid it in the pocket of her apron and got a fresh spoon from the sideboard before she placed the chairs for aunt and uncle and herself.

"You 'bout ready, Dora?" her aunt called from the kitchen.

"Yes, Aunt Jude. I don't see anything of Uncle Dan yet. Someone must have come in for a prescription."

She stepped into the parlor and glanced through the curtained window. The street was deserted. Mescal seemed to drowse under a warm noonday sun. Her attention went first to the lodge room above the firehouse, the town's only meeting place, where, at two o'clock that afternoon, she was to appear before the commissioners of the Willow Creek District School who were to act on her application for the position of teacher. *The worst they can do is to say no,* she thought.

A faint flush of excitement gave color to her cheeks today. Never having been exposed to a long Arizona summer, with its blinding sunshine and strong winds, her skin had lost none of its fresh, creamy loveliness since her arrival in Mescal, late in October. She had a good chin and mouth and intelligent blue eyes. In speaking of Eudora, however, other women oftener referred to her as sweet, rather than pretty.

The familiar figure of her uncle, a short, rotund, and jolly little man, careless of his clothes, appeared on the sidewalk. Old Gyp, a liver-colored hound, whose daily exercising was limited to following his master from the front porch to the drugstore six times a day, padded along behind him.

Eudora smiled fondly to herself as she watched them, thinking again how much her Uncle Dan and old Gyp had in common.

Neither had a mean bone in him. Other dogs might snarl and fight, but Gyp never permitted his curiosity to embroil him in their quarrels. Having demonstrated that he could not be induced into taking sides or engaging in strife and conflict seemed to have won him the respect of his canine world, and his rights were seldom invaded. The same could be said for Dan Stoddard. Through all the trouble that had plagued the basin, he not only had never allowed himself to become a partisan of either faction but, unlike Dad Beazley and other professed neutrals, had refused to be drawn into any discussion regarding it. He either had a good word to say of a man, or nothing at all. It followed that both stockman and home-steader held Dan Stoddard in high esteem.

"I'm a couple minutes late," he said, as Eudora opened the door for him. "Mrs. Bascom came in just as I was about to close up for noon." He sniffed at the appetizing odor that filled the house. "Fried chicken, eh! I thought I smelled it, coming up the walk. I'm here, Jude!" he called to his wife. "I was just telling Dora Mrs. Bascom came in and held me up a few minutes."

Mrs. Stoddard came to the kitchen door. She was a birdlike little woman, with quick, darting movements. "Someone sick at the Bascoms, Dan'l?"

"No, she just wanted some red cinnamon drops to color the frosting on a cake. It's been quite a morning in town."

"I should think so, and in more ways than one!" the little woman declared pointedly. Her eyes snapped disapprovingly in her thin face. "And I'm not speaking about the action the Association took. I needed some sugar. Dora was dressing, so I ran down to the market myself. Webb Nichols and Shad Caney were in a crowd in front of the blacksmith shop and ready to tear each other to pieces. They'd have fought if Virgil Hume hadn't got them apart."

"Shucks, Jude, you shouldn't pay any attention to one of their arguments," Dan protested, with a chuckle. "They like to blow off steam. But it doesn't mean anything. By and large, Webb and Shad are all right."

"Dan'l, don't you dare to stand there and try to defend those men to me!" Mrs. Stoddard exclaimed indignantly. "That Shad Caney is a lawless, bloodthirsty ruffian, and Webb Nichols isn't much better! The idea of electing such men to a school board! My blood runs cold when I think of Dora taking that school and living at the Nichols's place!"

"Now, don't take on," he protested, as he removed his coat. "I don't think you've got anything to worry about. They've had other teachers at Willow Creek and I never heard tell of them having any trouble."

"They've never had a young, inexperienced girl like Dora out there! I don't know what you call trouble, but I've heard Myra Krumbine say that in all the years she was teaching she never had such a time as at Willow Creek. Those Nichols and Caney children was fighting every day, even the little girls. Myra says they been raised like heathen. That oldest Nichols boy— Verne, they call him—is almost man-grown. There's one of the Caneys who's just as big. I don't see how Dora is going to handle them. I tell you, Dan'l, the more I think about it, the less I like the idea. I wisht I'd put my foot down in the first place!"

"Please, Aunt Jude, don't feel that way," Eudora pleaded. "Getting the school means so much to me. I couldn't withdraw my application now, even if I wanted to."

"Huh! I don't know why not; you ain't obligated yourself any. You sit down, Dan'l. Dora can bring the things in. I'll brown the gravy, and we can eat."

Mr. Stoddard sat down at his accustomed place and buttered a piece of bread. When Eudora came in from the kitchen with the fried chicken and the potatoes, he beckoned for her to bend down.

"Don't let Jude discourage you," he whispered.

"You'll make out all right. John Ringe stopped in a few minutes ago. He told me there wasn't any question about your being appointed."

He pinched her cheek affectionately. Eudora was his dead sister Eliza's only child. In the long ago, on a visit back to Ohio, he had seen her as a tot of two or three, and not again until the morning she stepped down from the Lund-Mescal stage. Left alone in the world, she had come to Arizona to make her home with Jude and him. Being childless themselves and set in their ways, they had received her with some misgiving. But Eudora had quickly taken complete possession of their hearts and filled their rather empty lives with exciting interest.

Mrs. Stoddard placed the gravy bowl and the coffeepot on the table. "I wanted to have a lemon pie for Dora, she's so fond of 'em, but there just isn't a lemon in town."

"I like apple pie just as well, Aunt Jude," said Eudora. "It looks wonderful."

Mrs. Stoddard shook her head. "I like an apple pie a bit juicy—I guess we can eat. You say grace, Dan'l."

They ate in silence for a few minutes. Dan glanced at his wife and saw her chin quiver as she kept her eyes on her plate.

"What is it, Jude?" he asked, solicitously.

"Our last meal together," she answered, dabbing at her eyes with her napkin. "How big this house is going to be again—just the two of us here."

"Why, I'll be coming into town, Aunt Jude," Eudora insisted. She reached across the table and gave the little woman's hand an affectionate squeeze. "I'll find a way. Mr. Nichols or someone will be driving in."

"Of course you will!" Dan agreed. "It ain't like you was going to the end of the world. The whole spring term is only ten weeks."

Mrs. Stoddard failed to find anything reassuring in their protestations. "It's almost forty miles out to Willow Creek!" she exclaimed, with a touch of irritation. "You know as well as I do, Dan'l, that if anyone comes in from out that way at this time of the year, they ain't likely to come in on a Saturday, when they've got their boys home from school and can get some work out of them. When she writes, it may be days before we get it, and our letters will most likely lay in the post office for ages. We won't know for weeks at a time how she is making out."

She was thoroughly aroused by now, and her mouth was a determined, resolute line.

"Dora, I'm going to speak real plain!" she declared. "You don't have to take that school because you're a burden on us. Your Uncle Dan'l can provide a living for his sister's only child. This is your home as much as it's ours.

Have we ever said anything to make you think otherwise?"

"Oh, Auntie, no!" Eudora cried. "Please don't think that! I've been so happy with you. It's only that I want to stand on my own feet. I know the Willow Creek school has its drawbacks; but it's a beginning for me. With some experience, I can get a better school next fall."

"You're right, Dora!" Mr. Stoddard said with an air of finality. When necessary, he could take a firm stand, and he was prepared to take one now. "I admire the spunk you're showing. I'm sure if you'll promise Jude that you won't try to stick it out if you find it's too much we won't have to say any more about it."

Eudora made the promise without examining it too closely. Mrs. Stoddard gave in reluctantly, but only after repeating several times that it was against what she called her "better judgment." The matter was too closely related to the action the stockmen's association had taken to be dismissed from their conversation completely.

"I suppose it's being discussed over every dinner table in town," Dan admitted, when he was pressed for his opinion regarding the latter step. "I don't believe any serious trouble will come of it. There's saner judgment on both sides than there used to be. It'll make itself felt."

"You don't believe anything of the sort," Mrs. Stoddard asserted reprovingly. "You know

35

there'll be trouble, and Webb Nichols and Shad Caney will be the first to get into it. You could go out on the street and ask a dozen men and they'd all tell you the same."

Dan shrugged patiently. "I was only giving you my opinion. I know Shad likes to keep a chip on his shoulder. Webb will do his share of talking, too. Feelings may run high for a time; but that's beside the point as far as Dora is concerned. If I thought she was going to be in any danger out there, I wouldn't let her go."

After dinner, it was his habit to doze for half an hour on the shaded front porch, with the faithful Gyp curled up at his feet. This noon, however, he said he would go back to the store at once, having several prescriptions to compound.

"Everybody likes to get away from town early," he said. "I'd let the dishes go, Jude, and give Dora a hand with her packing."

"Seems senseless to pack a trunk till she knows for certain she's going," Mrs. Stoddard replied. "If Mr. Ringe wants her, the other two are apt to vote no just for meanness."

Dan chuckled as he started for the door. "They might at that if they didn't need a teacher in a hurry. Dora won't be up there ten minutes."

His prediction was borne out, and with something to spare. Despite the bitter enmity the commissioners for the Willow Creek School

District bore one another, they could, when necessity demanded, rise above their differences. Webb and Caney studied Eudora furtively as she answered John Ringe's perfunctory questions. Big John left it to one of the others to indicate what their decision was to be.

"Wal, Miss Stoddard, you look and sound smart enough to teach a bunch of young uns their three R's," Webb spoke up, vaguely embarrassed by his own ignorance. "If you figger you can pound a little plain l'arnin' into their heads—and I mean pound—I'm for hirin' you."

The big cowman from the Santa Bonita nodded approvingly. "You're young, Miss Stoddard, and you haven't any experience, but I think you'll make out all right if you just take a firm stand with the older boys." He glanced at Caney. "How do you feel about it?"

"I'll go along with you if the young woman understands she ain't to play no favorites," said Shad. "I don't ask no special treatment for my young uns, nor am I goin' to have the teacher sidin' ag'in 'em, either." He fixed his baleful eyes on Eudora. "I want to make it plain to you, Miz Stoddard, that what happens outside the schoolyard ain't none of yore bizness."

Eudora was startled, and frightened too. She saw Webb bristling. One of the strongest arguments her aunt had used against her taking the position was the fact that the feud between the two men had been transmitted to their children, of which no less than six attended the Willow Creek school. Even the little girls fought at every opportunity.

"Mr. Ringe tells me I must assert my authority; you seem to advise the opposite course, Mr. Caney," she said, trying to hide her nervousness. "It's rather confusing. But as for being fair, I shall try to treat all the pupils alike—if that is what you mean."

It was only partly what Shad meant. He had always objected to the fact that the school was so situated that only Webb could provide bed and board for the teacher, for which he was reimbursed by the county. But aside from envying him the few dollars he made out of the arrangement, what really rankled in Shad's heart was the feeling that it gave the Nichols children an advantage over his own.

"My children was brought up to look out for themselves!" Webb growled. "They don't need no one takin' their part!"

"Let's get down to business!" big John boomed. "If we're going to split hairs over where Miss Stoddard's authority begins and ends, we might as well close the school. It's a waste of time to try to run it without discipline, and the only way she's going to get it is for this board to give her its full support."

Webb nodded soberly. "I'll go along with you on that."

"So do I!" Shad declared fiercely. "I jest want the school run right!"

Having reached an accord, however grudgingly, it did not take long to settle the other details. Eudora thanked them and hurried down the stairs. But now that the school was hers, she was filled with misgiving, rather than the expected elation.

But I can't back out, she thought. *I told Mr. Nichols I'd be ready to leave in an hour. Maybe it won't be as bad as I think.* Her mouth tightened resolutely. *I'm not going to let Aunt Jude see I'm upset. She'd worry herself sick!*

Though Mrs. Stoddard accepted her story without questions, she was not completely deceived. Several times Eudora glanced up, as she packed her trunk, to catch her aunt regarding her with an obscure concern.

"What is it, Auntie?" she was moved to ask. "Why do you look at me like that?"

Mrs. Stoddard pressed her thin lips together firmly. "I don't know, Dora," she declared dubiously. "You've got what you wanted, but somehow it strikes me you ain't as happy about it as you pretend."

"You're mistaken, Aunt Jude!" Eudora insisted. "I'm a little nervous, I guess. But I'll be all right after a day or two."

"Well, I hope so." The little woman shook her head. "John Ringe knows how to be a gentleman. But those other two—especially that Shad Caney—have got none of what you might call the finer instincts. Did they have words, Dora, and lay the law down to you?"

"No," Eudora lied bravely, "they were very considerate. They promised me I would have the full support of the board."

"Huh!" Mrs. Stoddard scoffed. "Precious little help you'll get! It's too bad the two of them didn't tear into each other as they usually do. It might have given you some idea of what you're letting yourself in for."

Webb was at the door a few minutes after Eudora had finished packing. He swung the small cowhide trunk over his shoulder and carried it out to his wagon. Eudora, looking very sedate in her little black bonnet, with its white ruching, and the long cape she had brought from Ohio, and Mrs. Stoddard followed him down the walk. The latter carried a shoe box, in which she had packed some cold fried chicken and other delicacies for Eudora's supper. "You shouldn't have bothered, Aunt Jude," the latter protested.

"It wasn't any bother, Dora. You'll be hungry later on. It'll be nine, ten o'clock before you get there. We'll just put the box under the seat."

Dan came out of the drugstore to see Eudora

off. He helped her into the wagon, after she had kissed Mrs. Stoddard and him good-by. Seated beside the towering Webb, she was a diminutive figure.

"I want you to take good care of her, Webb," Dan said.

Webb nodded. "Reckon she won't have as good as she's been used to, but we'll make her as comfortable as we can. Guess we can be movin'." He slapped the horses across the rump with ends of the reins. "G'dap there, Ben! Whup you, Bess!"

The wagon rolled away, with Eudora turning on the seat to wave to the old couple until Webb swung into the rutted dirt road that led eastward across the basin to Willow Creek. Eudora lowered her head. Out of the corner of his eye Webb saw her wipe away a tear.

"Nice folks, the Stoddards," he said, and then lapsed into a silence that held until Mescal had been left far behind.

Eudora had never been so far from town before. The tawny ribbon of road wound on endlessly through a land so vast that the jogging gait at which the team traveled seemed to make no impression on distance. Overhead, the sky was a cloudless blue canopy, stretching away to infinity. She gazed at it in awed silence, feeling she was just a mote, swimming in space. Her little worries and concerns fell

41

away from her and seemed to be of no consequence.

The air was heavy with the pungent fragrance of young sage. Unconsciously, she breathed deep of its clean, invigorating perfume. The westering sun was splashing Monument Butte and the ragged rimrock on Hurricane Ledge with vermilion and gold. Far to the east, the snow-capped peaks of the Desolation Mountains were so dwarfed by distance that they appeared to be only tufts of white cotton.

Somehow, the magnitude and magnificence of this wild land gave her strength and a strange sense of peace. She stole a glance at Webb, wondering if he still felt the tug of its beauty. He seemed to doze as he drove, but, to her surprise, he said, "It's even purtier in the mornin' when the sun is gittin' up. It'd be a nice country if there was more water. You'll be needin' that wrap in another hour; it gits cool in the basin of an evenin'."

Eudora mentioned the supper in the shoe box and asked him if he would share it with her.

"If there's enough for two, I'd take a bite," he observed.

They ate as they drove along. Webb lost some of his taciturnity. "My wife sets a good table," he volunteered. "Nothin' fancy, but there's allus plenty of what there is. She'll have yore lunch ready for you every mornin'."

"The school is some distance away?" Eudora inquired.

" 'Bout a mile and half. Just nice walkin' distance. When the weather gits bad, I'll git you there and back."

She asked about the cabin that was to be her home.

"It sits across the yard from the house," Webb told her. "Rheba—that's my wife—and the girls give it a good cleanin' last week. I'll take down the stove for you next month, when the nights git a little warmer. You don't have to be afraid of nothin' botherin' you."

It was all very reassuring to Eudora. The sun went down and the purple haze of twilight descended on the basin. It was a magic hour. But the purple faded to a fearsome slate gray and the sagebrush lost its greenish hue and looked dead and ghostly in the afterglow. Whippoorwills sailed over it, with their mournful, monotonous cry. Then, suddenly it was night. Off in the malpais, a coyote yelped disconcertingly. Eudora moved closer to Webb. The world had lost its grandeur and bigness.

She pulled her cape about her as the night wind sprang up and a chill crept into the air. The team plodded on. At long intervals, a buttery daub of light from a window marked the site of a homesteader's cabin.

It was after nine o'clock when they came to

a flowing stream. Halfway across, Webb pulled up and let the horses drink.

"Willow Crick," he said, breaking a long silence. "She swings back and forth considerable. We'll cross her three times before we git home. 'Bout eight mile to go."

They left the creek and were moving toward the second crossing, when flashes of fire stabbed the blackness in the creek bottom ahead of them and the unmistakable thunder of guns rolled up to their ears. Webb straightened up instantly and tightened his grip on the reins. Eudora huddled close to him and caught his arm.

"Mr. Nichols, that was gunfire!" she cried, her throat tight with alarm. "There are two more shots!"

The shooting was farther away now.

"It's a gun fight, all right!" Webb got out gruffly. He listened intently, but the night was still again.

"What does it mean?" Eudora asked in a very small voice. "Are such things a common occurrence out here?"

"I don't know what it means," he answered gruffly. "Whatever it is, it don't concern you. If you hear or see things you don't understand, don't try to find out what they mean. Yore job is to teach school, Miss Stoddard —nothin' else!"

Chapter Four

In a Bit of a Fix

Though the long ride had tired her Eudora spent a restless night. The cabin was clean, and if plainly furnished, not too uncomfortable. She could give it a few little touches, she thought, that would make it livable. But it was strange, and the creaking of the roof and rattling of the windows, as well as the night sounds without, kept her wide-eyed and apprehensive. The Nichols's chickens brought the coyotes in close to the yard. Once, the shrill, hideous yipping seemed to come from just beyond the window at the foot of her bed. She buried her face in the pillow and lay there trembling.

"This is foolish!" she told herself. "I've got to get used to it. No one in Arizona bothers about a coyote."

It was such a sound argument that it tended to quiet her fears in that direction. She could find no comparable logic to ease her mind in regard to those blazing guns in the Willow Creek bottoms, however, and it was that sinister and unexplained cracking of rifles in the blackness

45

of the night that was at the bottom of her anxiety and nervousness.

The shots had been so spaced that she knew instinctively that there had been a fight. She believed Webb had spoken the truth when he said he didn't know what it meant, or who was a party to it. But the sharpness of the admonition he had given her, and his refusal to say anything further, thereafter, indicated plainly enough that he wasn't totally in the dark.

Eudora fell asleep just before dawn, but it seemed she had barely closed her eyes before she heard the younger Nichols children playing in the yard. Shyness, or a parental command, kept them away from the cabin. They trooped in to breakfast before she finished dressing.

It was a clean blue and white morning, the sun pleasantly warm, the air invigorating. Eudora's spirits lifted and she smiled ruefully over having spent such an uneasy night.

"I won't go to pieces like that again," she promised herself. "I'm going to love this high country."

A line of willows and heavy buckbrush plainly marked the twisting course of Willow Creek. It looked so peaceful in the morning sunshine that she wondered if her imagination hadn't enlarged on the violence of the clash in the bottoms, the previous evening.

The road that continued eastward across the basin was just a beaten path through the sagebrush. Eudora's glance followed it as she started across the yard. In the distance, she could see the schoolhouse. It looked small. But so did the house and barn, for the country had been fashioned on such a grand scale that whatever man built seemed tiny and inadequate.

Having spent several years of her childhood on an Ohio farm, she looked about her with interest. Save for the chickens and the truck patch down by the creek, she found little that was familiar. Beyond the barn, there was a pole corral, decorated by several coyote pelts that had been hung up to dry. A young cottonwood, its catkins just beginning to swell, raised its head outside the kitchen door, where it obviously had the benefit of the daily dishwater. It was the only tree in the yard. But it was the absence of the usual litter of farm tools and machinery, rather than the lack of living green things, that she missed most.

The truth was that Webb had little need for anything beyond a plow and mowing machine, which were carefully kept under cover, for 40 acres of alfalfa hay was the only crop he took from the soil; his cows ranged over the rest of his original quarter section and the 80 acres he had acquired recently.

The kitchen door stood open and Eudora

saw that the family was at the table. At that moment, a shaggy dog, of uncertain parentage, came running from the direction of the barn and set up a great barking. It brought a teen-aged boy to the door. He picked up a stick and brandished it at the dog.

"Stop that, Bruno!" he yelled. "Go on!"

The dog slunk away, and the boy turned to Eudora, jerking up his head to toss his tawny, unkempt hair back from his face. Young as he was, he was almost a six-footer. She correctly surmised that he was Verne Nichols, Webb's oldest son. "He makes a lot of noise, but he won't bite, less you tease him," he said, self-consciously.

Webb shouldered him aside. "Come in, Miss Stoddard," he invited. "We just set down."

Mrs. Nichols got up as Eudora stepped into the kitchen. "Laws, Miss, you didn't need to git up so early!" she exclaimed, apologetically. "If you hear us stirrin', don't pay no attention to it. The teacher can have her breakfast as late as seven o'clock."

"It's such a beautiful morning that I'm glad to be up early," Eudora assured her. "I thought I'd walk over to the school and get things ready for Monday."

The two younger children, Elly, a dark-eyed girl of eight, who strongly resembled her mother, and Hagar, a tot of three or four, were giggling

48

nervously. Verne and his brother Moroni, two years his junior, continued eating, but they stole furtive glances at Eudora.

"Moroni, you slide over on the bench with the girls and give Miss Stoddard yore chair," Webb ordered, his tone leaving no doubt that when he spoke he was to be obeyed. "The key to the schoolhouse is hangin' there beside the door," he told Eudora. "You take charge of it."

Mrs. Nichols brought Eudora's breakfast from the stove. She was younger than Webb, but hard work had left its mark on her hands and face and made her look old beyond her years. She sat down after filling Eudora's cup and ate a mouthful or two.

"My, you *are* young to be out teachin'!" she observed, studying Eudora with frank interest. "Maybe you'll git along better with the children on that account. When a woman gits to be an old maid, she gits so set in her ways that all the patience dries out of her and she don't understand young folks. When I was goin' to school, I always got more learnin' from young teachers."

Eudora smiled at this bit of homely philosophy and said she hoped it would hold true in her case.

"I see no reason why it won't," Mrs. Nichols told her. "Of course, the trouble with attractive young wimmen like you is that yo're always runnin' off and gittin' married, and that's the end of the teachin'.'"

She recalled an incident of her girlhood in Utah to prove her point. She seemed happy to have someone of her own sex to whom she could talk. Webb gave her a glance, however, and she fell silent.

Trivial as the incident was, it confirmed Eudora's feeling that Rheba Nichols was only the family drudge; that authority rested solely in Webb. Proof of it came a few minutes later, when Elly asked Eudora if she could accompany her to the schoolhouse.

"Elly, you talk too much!" Verne said, with a reprimanding scowl. "Miss Stoddard don't want to be bothered with you."

The little girl ignored him and appealed to her father. "May I, Papa?"

Webb was ready to say no, when Eudora told him she would be happy to have Elly go with her. "I may be there several hours, but I'll send her home as soon as she's shown me where I can find everything."

Webb considered. "If she can help you any, she can go."

No one asked Mrs. Nichols what she thought about it.

The shooting had not been mentioned, and though Elly chattered like a magpie as she tried to keep step with Eudora on the long walk to the schoolhouse, she made no reference to it. Eudora was above trying to draw her out, though she suspected the child wasn't totally ignorant about it. She found the youngster's prattling enlightening, not to say disturbing, when it touched on the Caney children.

"You're too nice a little girl, Elly, to be saying such dreadful things," she protested firmly. "I'm not acquainted with Cissy Caney, but she can't be as mean and wicked as you say."

"Yes, she is, Miss Stoddard!" Elly insisted. "I hate all them Caneys!"

"All those Caneys," Eudora corrected.

"All those Caneys," Elly parroted. "The whole pack of them tell lies and cheat. Verne says they'll steal the pennies off a dead man's eyes if they get the chance. But I'm not afraid of Cissy, less she's got Lorenzo and that big Jeb to help her."

"Elly, do you mean to tell me the three of them attacked you?" Eudora demanded incredulously.

"Right in the schoolyard! They knocked me down and Cissy pulled my hair something awful. But Verne laid for 'em and gave Jeb and Lorenzo a good punching."

Eudora knew she was venturing on dangerous ground in offering advice, but she refused to remain silent. It made her blood run cold to see how the feud between Webb Nichols and Shad had poisoned the minds of their children.

"The thing for you to do, Elly, is to go straight home from school. You won't have any trouble if you do." Elly would have contradicted her, but she said, "Let me finish! There's always two sides to every story. When the Caney children come to me with their side of it, I'll give them the same advice I'm giving you. I won't permit any of you to loiter around the schoolhouse after class has been dismissed. Nor will there be any quarreling in the yard at the noon recess. If there is, whoever takes part in it will be sent home promptly. And they won't be allowed back until they have convinced me they mean to behave themselves. I want to make things as pleasant as I can for all of you, but you children will have to do your part."

She realized Elly was very young to be spoken to so seriously. She felt certain, however, that the little girl would repeat their conversation to her brothers, and she had spoken with that in mind, feeling she had been given an opportunity to make her position known that was not to be missed.

Elly had begun to lose some of her enthusiasm for her new teacher. The laughter had faded from her eyes and the expression that settled on her mouth was sullen. Eudora put an arm about the child's shoulders and gave her an affectionate little hug. Pretending not to be aware of the pouting lips, she said, "I'm sure you'll help me, Elly, and that will mean a lot to me. But we won't say anything more about it; it's too nice a morning for us to be troubling our heads with such things. Do you know the song about the gingerbread boy who jumped out of the cooky jar?"

"I know part of it," Elly answered, without looking up.

"Suppose you sing it with me," Eudora urged. "It's a jolly song. Hold out your hand— First a pit, and then a pat."

Elly knew the song well enough, and Eudora soon had her laughing and smiling again.

When they reached the schoolhouse, they found the front door smeared with dried blood. The carcass of a dead jack rabbit lay on the ground beside the steps.

"I bet Jeb Caney did it!" Elly declared at once. "Their place is only a couple of miles east of Jerusalem Crick. When he's out hunting, he comes this way."

Eudora bit her lips. "I'll get some soap and water and give the door a scrubbing."

She found the appointments of the school less primitive than she expected. Elly knew where everything was to be found, from the bell to the closet where the broom and dustpan were kept.

Eudora rolled up her sleeves and put on an apron. "I'll scrub that door before I do anything else!" she said, more to herself than Elly.

The latter took a bucket out to the well and filled it. Armed with a stiff brush and soap, Eudora soon had the door clean and shining. Elly laughed as she saw her looking askance at the dead rabbit. Without any ado, she picked it up by its long ears and tossed it over the fence. "There's nothing about a rabbit that'll hurt you, Miss Stoddard."

Eudora shuddered. "I don't suppose there is," she admitted. "But you go to the pump and wash your hands, Elly. And then you had better be starting back. I promised your father—"

"Can't I clean the blackboard before I go?" the youngster pleaded.

"Yes, you may. But then you'll have to go."

When Elly left, Eudora stood on the steps and watched her tripping down the road. *I suppose Aunt Jude would call her a little savage,* she thought, and shook her head. *I'm going to like Elly.*

For half an hour, she busied herself rearranging her desk. She felt singularly self-possessed as she sat there alone in the empty schoolroom. She filled the seats with imaginary pupils and pretended to address them in a silent rehearsal of what she would say on Monday morning.

Even with the sunshine streaming through the windows, the room was drab.

The first time I go into Mescal, I must remember to clip some pictures from the magazines, she thought. *Some gay prints will brighten the walls, I'll get some geranium slips from Aunt Jude too. Flowers in the windows are always cheerful.*

Her predecessor had left a record of the work that had been accomplished up to the close of the last term. Seventeen pupils had attended the Willow Creek school during the winters, the majority of them in the lower grades.

The frequent erasures in the report made it hard to follow and seemed to indicate some confusion in the mind of the compiler.

I shouldn't wonder! Eudora thought. *Teaching four grades in one room could confuse anyone.*

She sat there struggling with it for some time, when she became conscious of a shadow at the west window. She looked up and was thoroughly startled to find a man peering in at her. As she stared at him helplessly, he left the window and she could hear him hurrying around to the door, where he took the key out of the lock. When he stepped in, he closed the door behind him.

Eudora had got to her feet, not knowing what to expect.

"You needn't be scared, ma'am," he said.

"Reckon I look purty tough this mornin', but don't let that bother you."

He had a crooked smile that Eudora found engaging, frightened though she was. His right arm hung helplessly by his side. Her eyes widened as she gazed at it.

"Your arm!" she exclaimed. "You've been shot!"

"It ain't nuthin' serious," he drawled. "You've got to do me a favor. I'm in a little bit of a fix— No, I don't mean bind up my arm. I want you to git out of here. There's some parties lookin' for me. They'll be comin' down the road in a few minutes. When they show up, I want you to step out and let 'em see you lockin' the door. You go on back to Nichols's place, then. These gents will ask you if you've seen me. I'll appreciate it, ma'am, if you tell 'em no."

From the moment he had entered, Eudora had found something faintly familiar about him. What he had said quickened her memory. Finally, she was sure.

"You're Steve Jennings, the rustler! I've seen your picture on the reward notices in Mescal!"

She felt her knees shaking.

"Yeh, I'm Steve Jennings, ma'am," he admitted, with a grin.

Chapter Five

An Observing Young Woman

The meaning of the gunfire she had witnessed on Willow Creek was no longer a mystery to Eudora.

She saw Jennings bite back a wince of pain.

"These boys who are hot on my trail are a bunch of Ringe's punchers. Is it goin' to do you any good to turn me over to 'em?" he asked. "The trouble between us don't concern you, ma'am."

"Why should you come to me for help?" she demanded, with rising indignation. "I've been warned by some members of the school board to mind my own business. I didn't know that included concealing their rustler friends."

Jennings grinned ruefully again. "I didn't mean it to happen this way. Reckon they didn't either. I made a mistake, comin' down the Wash in broad daylight. Big John's boys spotted me and kinda upset my plans."

"You'll come to a horrible end," Eudora said firmly. "I understand there's a price on you in several states. If I helped you now I wouldn't have the excuse of thinking I was giving you a chance to get away and make a fresh start. You haven't any intention of changing your ways."

Steve's smile faded and his face fell into sober lines. "I reckon that's right," he drawled. "It's a little late for me to be changin' my ways. The law's got too many grudges ag'in me."

Eudora gazed at him pityingly. In his faded overalls and sweat-stained Stetson, this tow headed man, with his winning smile, bore little resemblance to the dangerous, cold-blooded outlaw of the stories she had heard.

"You can't escape on foot." She wasn't aware of it, but her tone was brusque, even scolding. "Where have you left your horse?"

"I had my bronc shot out from under me last night, a couple miles down the crick." He jerked his head to indicate his wounded arm. "That's where I got that."

"So it was you!" Eudora charged. "I thought so!"

Jennings's eyes puckered questioningly. "How did you know anythin' about it, ma'am?"

Her explanation satisfied him. He had watched the road as he talked. Suddenly, he reached with his left hand and got his gun out of the holster. Eudora felt her throat tighten.

"You better git down on the floor," he advised grimly. "They're comin', and there's shore to be some shootin'."

"You fool!" she cried. "You wouldn't have a chance—four against one! You get into this closet, so they won't see you if they look in. I'll lie for you this once; but don't expect it of me a second time."

"There won't be another time if I can help it," Steve answered, with his winning smile. "And thank you, ma'am!"

Eudora whipped off her apron and stepped out. The four horsemen coming up the road were less than 100 yards away. Pretending to be unaware of them, she locked the door carefully, making sure they saw her. Amazed that she could be so calm, she went down the path and started walking in their direction. The four men reined in as she approached.

Eudora greeted them with an impersonal smile. She remembered having seen at least two of them on the street in Mescal at various times.

"Just a minute, ma'am," one interjected, as she would have continued on her way. "Yo're Dan Stoddard's niece and the new teacher yere, ain't you?"

Eudora acknowledged that this was so.

"How long you been at the school this mornin', Miss Stoddard?"

"I—I don't know. Several hours, I should think," Eudora replied, managing to hide her nervousness. "Why do you ask?"

"We're lookin' fer Steve Jennings," said the puncher. "We know he ain't far ahead of us. Have you seen anyone lurkin' around here? He's wounded; we don't know how bad."

"Steve Jennings!" Eudora exclaimed in a shocked voice, her real and pretended alarm blending convincingly. "I'm sure I wouldn't have remained here a minute if I had seen him. I thought I heard someone ride past some time ago. I was busy, so I didn't go to the window."

"It's what I told yuh, Cleve," a second man spoke up. "Nichols has fixed him up with a hoss."

Cleve shook his head. "I don't believe it! We had him cut off in that direction. He's most likely makin' for Caney's place." He touched his hat and gave Eudora an admiring glance. "I'm sorry we bothered you, Miss Stoddard. If you run into Steve, you don't have to worry about him harmin' you none. I reckon you could capture him without half tryin'."

Eudora gazed at him blankly, pretending not to have heard the compliment. He kneed his horse and jogged off with his companions. It was all she could do to keep from glancing back as she continued on her way. She heard them pull their horses to a walk at the school; but after a moment's hesitation, they went on. Her taut nerves began to relax, and she breathed a sigh of relief. Now that the ordeal was over, she felt weak and exhausted.

Webb and Verne were not at the table at noon. Mrs. Nichols said they were working in the north pasture and might not be in until late. Elly and her brother Moroni seemed strangely quiet and restrained. It made Eudora wonder if they had some inkling of what had happened at the schoolhouse and had been charged not to mention it. As for herself, she had resolved to say nothing unless Webb, or one of the family, brought it up.

With the long afternoon ahead of her, she unpacked her trunk and rearranged the cabin to her liking. Her mind was preoccupied with Steve Jennings and the possible consequences of what she had done. A dozen times she stopped at the window and gazed at the schoolhouse, wondering if he had opened a window and let himself out, or if he was still hiding there, waiting for darkness to cover his escape. She realized if her part in it ever became known it was sure to win her the unremitting hostility of John Ringe.

And I was going to be so careful not to become involved! she thought reproachfully. *But I don't know what else I could have done. He was wounded; I didn't want to see him killed before my eyes.*

Elly came over about five o'clock with the freshly ironed curtains.

"Come in and help me put them up," Eudora

urged. "I've moved the furniture around a bit. Tell me how you like it, Elly."

"It looks real pretty," the little girl declared. "None of the other teachers ever bothered much about fixing things up."

Elly seemed as friendly as ever, but Eudora couldn't help feeling the child was mindful of what she talked about. She was delighted with a pale blue ribbon Eudora gave her.

"I wisht I could wear it in my hair tomorrow," Elly said. "But Mormons don't wear bright colors to church. Elder Whitman says vanity in a woman is sinful."

Eudora was glad her head was turned so she could smile. "You can wear it to school next week," she told Elly. "A little girl can have pretty things without being vain. I'm sure Elder Whitman would agree with me. I didn't know there was a Mormon church in the basin. Where is it located, Elly?"

"Down White Pine way. But it isn't really a church or meeting house, Miss Stoddard. It's just Elder Whitman's barn. When the weather is fine, he has services in his yard." She glanced toward the house with sudden uneasiness. "I better be going before I get a scolding; I've got to gather eggs."

"That sounds like fun," Eudora exclaimed. "Do you mind if I come along?"

Elly's eyes brightened. "Sure you can come!

You better not go into the hen house, though; it's awful dirty. I'll run to the house and get my basket."

As they walked down the yard together Eudora saw Webb disappearing into the barn. He was carrying a kettle of water, so hot, steam was rising from it. Verne sat in the barn's wide doorway, oiling a piece of harness. He smiled timidly at Eudora and followed her with his eyes as she passed.

Bruno, the dog, barked at them as they neared the woodshed.

"Verne says he won't bite," Eudora remarked.

"He won't," Elly agreed. "You can pet him if you let him smell your hand first."

They stopped, and Eudora quickly made friends with the dog. "I hope they haven't chained you up on my account, Bruno."

"No, we got to keep him chained for a couple days," Elly explained. "Verne set out some baits for the coyotes this afternoon. Papa says they're getting too thick for anything."

The corral that had been empty that morning now held half a dozen horses. Eudora wondered if one of them, by any chance, was for Steve Jennings.

After peering into the littered hen house, she decided to take Elly's advice to remain outside. With amused interest she watched the antics of a scolding White Leghorn hen and her scurrying brood. Two roosters got into an altercation. Eudora laughed at the haughty disdain with which the old hen ignored them.

Elly had her basket filled when she came out. Eudora offered to carry it. "It's been a long while since I carried a basketful of eggs," she said.

Going up the yard, they passed close to the open barn door. An unmistakably carbolic odor reached Eudora's nostrils. Hot water and a carbolic disinfectant would be used to treat a gunshot wound. The thought leaped through her mind that Steve Jennings had made his way to the barn; that Webb was caring for him and had posted Verne at the entrance to stand guard.

She sniffed to let Elly know she had caught the odor, and said innocently, "Your father must have a sick animal on his hands."

"Pshaw! We don't keep the stock in the barn," the youngster said without thinking. The words were no sooner out, however, than she seemed to realize she had made a slip. "You say the strangest things, Miss Stoddard!" she complained, and had no more to say.

It was enough for Eudora; she was certain beyond any doubt that Steve Jennings was in the barn.

There was very little conversation at the table that evening. Webb remarked that he had put in a hard day, but at what, he didn't say. Mrs. Nichols looked weary, and her labors were not finished. As soon as supper was over, Verne picked up a pair of folded towels and wrapped them around a bar of soap. "Come on," he said to Moroni.

"Gee, I bet the water's cold!" Elly exclaimed as the two boys started for the creek and the weekly Saturday-night bath.

"Cold for sissy girls, I guess!" Moroni retorted, his tone expressing how disdainful he was of the comparative luxury Elly and little Hagar enjoyed of warm water in a washtub on the kitchen floor.

Webb told Eudora they were driving to White Pine in the morning and would be leaving early.

"There's no need of yo're gittin' up, Miss Stoddard," Mrs. Nichols said. "That is, if you don't mind gittin' yore own breakfast. You can come over whenever you git ready."

Eudora thanked her. "But if I happen to be up before you leave, don't bother about me," she urged. "I know you'll be anxious to get started."

She felt sure that sometime during the night Steve Jennings would emerge from the barn and ride away on one of Webb's horses. She lay awake long after she went to bed, listening. She fell asleep, however, without hearing

65

anything to confirm her conclusion. She felt more at home and not even the yipping of the coyotes disturbed her. When the banging of the kitchen door awakened her, she glanced at her watch and found it was past six o'clock. Her eyes went to the corral at once. It held only five horses this morning.

When Webb left the house and hurried down to the barn, she opened the windows for the double purpose of letting in the warm morning sunshine and informing him she was awake. It incensed her to think, in view of the help she had given Jennings, that Webb found it necessary to employ such elaborate secrecy against her.

It isn't as though Mrs. Nichols and the rest of the family didn't know all about it, she thought.

She was dressed by the time he had the team hitched. He drove up to the house and put the family in the wagon. He started to get in with them, only to check himself and turn toward the cabin.

Eudora let him knock before she went to the door.

"We may not be back till two, three o'clock," he said. "I was just thinkin' you might be a bit scary about stayin' here alone, though there's no reason why you should be."

"I don't suppose there is," Eudora admitted.

"But I think I'd feel better if I had a gun—just in case a wounded outlaw happened to be concealed in the barn," she added coolly.

Webb understood her perfectly, and she intended he should. His head went up and he regarded her sternly for a moment.

"Yo're a very observin' young woman, Miss Stoddard."

"Is that all you have to say?" she inquired thinly.

"There may be some things I'd prefer you not to know," he replied, with lowered brows. "But I can guarantee you there's no one in the barn this mornin'. I hope that satisfies you; you showed yesterday that you know how to use yore head."

"Then, you knew about it, Mr. Nichols."

Webb nodded woodenly. "I ain't unappreciative, Miss Stoddard, but it's somethin' you'll do well to forgit."

Chapter Six

The Lynching

Clay Roberts, the stock-detective, slipped into Mescal quietly and was met by John Ringe and Coconino Williams. After leaving town with them, he dropped out of sight. According to the gossip in the basin, he was making his headquarters with Big John on the Santa Bonita.

Though the trouble that had been so freely predicted would follow his coming had not materialized, there had been no noticeable lessening of tension among the homesteaders and small ranchers. Even Harvey Hume and his friends, who felt that violence could and should be avoided, shared the general feeling that something would happen to end the uneasy calm. On successive Sundays, following the service at Elder Whitman's, the Mormon contingent had spoken of little else. Webb Nichols, and several others, had urged taking a firm and united stand and making their decision known to Ringe and his associates. The Humes had mustered support enough to defeat the proposal; but no one saw in this refusal to take action any reason for relaxing his watchfulness.

The weather had turned warm and the lower passes and the Ledge were free of snow. Usually, it meant an outbreak of rustling. But there were no reports of stock being run off. It was incredible, and to no one more than to young Harvey. "There'll be rustling this spring, and we'll hear of it any day, now," he often told himself.

He was so sure of it that whenever he saw a neighbor riding in he fully expected him to be bringing that very news.

This afternoon, he was down at the milking corral, repairing the gate that an amorous bull had knocked down, when his uncle Virgil rode across the unfenced range that lay between their places. Being next-door neighbors, so to speak, they saw a great deal of each other. But Virgil had so little liking for the saddle that he always drove over, though it meant coming around by way of the road, unless he had something urgent on his mind.

He's heard something! Harvey thought, as he waited.

Virgil was so heavy it took a big horse to carry him. He grunted as he got down.

"Well, it's happened!" he announced. "Caney's done what he threatened to do! He's brought in sheep!"

Harvey's mouth lost its tightness. "I thought you had some important news—"

"About Roberts?"

"Yeh."

Virgil shook his head. "What I'm tellin' you is important enough! Where's Caney goin' to run sheep? He can't put them on his own range unless he gits rid of his cows. He's got as many head as I have, and less graze. I couldn't put sheep on my place."

"How he manages it is up to him," Harvey declared complacently. "I know there's feeling against sheep, but if he wants them, I guess that's his business. He's far enough away so that what he does won't hurt us."

"Harvey, how can you stand there and talk like that?" Virgil demanded irascibly. "You got good sense in you about most things. Why are you so dumb about this? You ought to know it won't be no time before them sheep will be beyond bounds. They don't want to swarm on that Government land between Caney's and the Santa Bonita line! Ringe has leased that range, and he won't stand for trespassin'. If they're turned back in that direction, they'll drift west and be on Nichols's range. Whichever way they go, there's shore to be trouble. And I mean trouble for all of us! I think Caney knows it and is doin' it deliberately!"

Harvey began to see the matter in a more serious light.

"That could be his way of forcing our hand," he said. "If Ringe's punchers catch the sheep trespassing and club the heads off a bunch of them, some folks will get worked about it. I don't know what we can do, Virgil; it would be a waste of breath to try to say anything to Shad."

They discussed the matter at length. Both were of the same opinion as to what would happen if the sheep were driven on Webb's range.

"He'll go gunnin' for Shad, shore as yo're standin' there!" Virgil asserted. "If he don't git him the first time, he'll keep at it till one or t'other of 'em is killed. I'm for Webb, first and last, in any argument he has with Caney. I reckon he can take care of himself. But if they start blazin' away at each other it'll be their own private fight, no matter how it turns out. That won't be the case if Ringe gits into it." The brawny man shook his head soberly. "Wait till Big John hears there's sheep just across his line!"

"Caney knows exactly how Ringe will feel. It may make Shad a little careful. After all, Virgil, if he's put what money he's got into sheep, he can't afford to have them killed, no matter what his game is."

Virgil rolled his shoulders noncommittally and had no immediate answer. But after thinking it over, he said, "You may have somethin' there, though he's the kind who's always ready to bite off their nose to spite their face. How's yore mother?"

"She's fine," Harvey told him. "She's been churning all afternoon. We're getting a good price for butter. If I could get someone to help her, I'd buy some more milkers."

Virgil nodded. "Butter shore brings in a few dollars. But I ain't complainin'; we're gittin' ahead slowly."

Harvey asked him about his family as they gathered up the tools.

"Ever'body's fine, Harvey. Josie is goin' back to school for the spring term. She's the only one from down this way attendin' at Willow Crick, so Mary has to fetch her back and forth. Four miles is too far for her to hoof it. Have you seen the new teacher?"

"I've seen her in town. She was in the drugstore one day when I was in. Mr. Stoddard introduced us. How is she making out?"

"Josie is crazy about her. She never wanted to go when Miss Krumbine was teachin'; now, she can't git there early enough. From what I gather, this Stoddard girl has got the whole school wrapped around her finger." Virgil chuckled. "Josie says that big lad of Caney's and Webb's boy Verne are sweet on the teacher."

"If that's the case, it may not turn out to be as amusing as you think," said Harvey. "Mix a little jealousy and calf love into the hatred those boys hold for each other and you're apt to have an explosion."

They walked back to the barn and sat down in the doorway. They had been there ten minutes or more, when Virgil stood up to get a better view of the horseman who was moving over the road in their direction. The main road across the basin ran by Harvey's house. Just beyond his place it put out one fork to the northeast and upper Willow Creek, and another in the direction of White Pine. As a consequence, he saw someone passing a dozen times a day.

"Who is it?" he asked.

"It's Frank Dufors. I thought I saw him goin' by early this mornin'. I suppose he's got somethin' important on his mind." Virgil's tone was sarcastic. "Accordin' to Webb, Dufors was all set to put Roberts in his place, but he didn't git the chance to do any blowin'. Roberts didn't bother to go near him. That must've burned Dufors."

Harvey let it pass without comment. "He sees us," he said. "Looks like he's going to turn in."

The deputy sheriff jerked a nod at them and jogged up to the barn. His manner was not too friendly. "Have you heard the news?" he asked, without getting down.

"What news?" Harvey inquired casually.

"About what happened at Parley Scott's place last evenin'."

Harvey and Virgil said no. Dufors regarded them with a smirking contempt. He knew the stand they had taken, and he relished being the one to reach them first with the news.

"It'll make the two of you change yore tune!" he predicted. "You've got a lot of folks to believin' there wouldn't be any trouble if they just held in a little. You won't git no one to swallow that after this. Roberts and most of Coconino Williams's crew rode into Parley's place about seven o'clock last night and took three men out of his house."

"Rustlers, eh?" Virgil inquired calmly.

"Yeh, rustlers! But Roberts and that bunch didn't have no legal right to bust into a man's home. That's what has got me riled. If they can get away with that they can do it to anyone. It could be yore turn next if—"

"Wait a minute," young Harvey put in. "How did Roberts happen to know the men he wanted were hiding there? Some stock been rustled?"

"That's what they say. Roberts laid a trap for Salazar, and the fool walked into it."

"So, it was Mescalero Joe!" Virgil observed. "Who was with him?"

"A couple of breeds. Roberts was hid out in

Little Cochinilla Wash and movin' around just enough to let 'em know he was there. They got past him and cut out a bunch of Williams's steers. They started hazin' 'em up to'ard the hot springs so as to give Roberts the slip. That's just what he figgered they'd do, and when they got to the springs, they ran into Williams's punchers. They dropped the cattle and made a run for it, after some shootin'. Parley says Salazar told him they'd shaken off all signs of 'em, just about sundown. That's why Parley agreed to take him in. I reckon Roberts joined up with the rest of the bunch, when he heard the shootin', and picked up Salazar's trail."

The failure of the Humes to grow excited over his tale angered Dufors. "But I tell you again it ain't Joe Salazar and the other two I'm talkin' about! A man's home is his castle, and even a law officer has to have a warrant, or purty near know what he's doin' before he can search a man's house!"

His voice had risen so violently that it brought Harvey's mother to the kitchen door. After looking out and seeing who was doing the talking, she went back to her work.

"Is that what Roberts did—search Parley's house?" Harvey asked.

"It's what he threatened to do!" Dufors exclaimed. "And he'd have done it if some-body hadn't found three hot broncs in the corral just then. Parley knew the jig was up, so he told Joe and the others to come out."

The Humes digested his tale silently for a few moments. "You're all worked up over this, Dufors," said Harvey. "I don't believe anyone else is going to take it so hard. It strikes me Roberts used his head. Someone could have taken a shot at Parley, or slapped him around; he knew he was sheltering rustlers who had been caught red-handed. He wasn't hurt any, I take it."

"No—o," Dufors admitted reluctantly. "But it's the principle of the thing that sticks in my craw!"

"The principle that you can hide a thief under yore bed and it's nobody's business?" Virgil demanded thinly. "That's the kind of talk we used to swallow. It doesn't go down so easy today. Mebbe Caney and some others will feel as you do about this business, but I figger it's the best thing could have happened. It makes it plain enough that it's the rustlers, not us, the Association and this man Roberts are out to smash. What did they do with Mescalero Joe and his friends?"

"I don't know!" Dufors growled. "They rode off with 'em."

"Wal, ain't it yore business to find out? Yo're the law."

"Don't try to tell me off!" the deputy sheriff

snapped. "What do you think I been doin'? I saw Williams, and I had it out with Roberts. They claimed there was nothin' they could tell me. Bill Rowan, Williams's foreman, was the only one who'd talk. He says they gave Joe and his pals a good hidin' and turned 'em loose."

"You believe it?" Virgil asked.

"Not for a minute! Rowan and the rest of 'em are just puttin' themselves in the clear. But it ain't up to me to do anythin' further till I got more to go on."

Virgil's smile was anything but respectful. "I figgered you'd be careful," he observed dryly.

What had happened to Mescalero Joe Salazar and his two partners did not remain a mystery for long. The storekeeper at White Pine took a day off and went hunting. He found what he was looking for where Cochinilla Wash and Little Cochinilla ran together. It was a favorite thoroughfare for rustlers moving down from the Desolations and Hurricane Ledge to ply their trade in the basin. His story spread rapidly, and a score of sightseers went up to view the grisly scene. The flapping buzzards and circling crowd led them to the spot.

Webb Nichols stopped at Harvey's place on his way back. He wore a grim look. "It's just as Adkins said—the three of 'em hangin' there in a row! You know that big cottonwood the lightnin' hit a couple summers back?" Harvey nodded.

"That's the place! It was a terrible sight! Parley got sick to the stomach and threw up." Webb shook his head pessimistically. "I don't know what we're goin' to do, Harvey! Some of us pullin' one way and some the other. They could've strung Parley up as easy as not."

"But they didn't, Webb. That's what you want to remember. We'll be all right if we mind our own business and get the idea out of our heads that we owe these rustlers any favors."

Webb regarded him closely, wondering if this was Harvey's way of telling him he knew about the help Steve Jennings had received.

"Rubbing out that bunch won't stop the rustling," Harvey continued. "Salazar was just small fry; it would be different if Steve Jennings had been strung up."

Webb tightened a cinch strap that wasn't in particular need of tightening. There was cold hostility in his narrowed eyes when he straightened up. "They'll never take Steve that way—not if he has half a chance to put his hand on a gun. What's behind yore throwin' him up to me? This is the second time you've done it."

"Don't get excited; nobody's throwing him up to you," Harvey replied, placatingly. "It's

78

picking him off by inches. His horse was killed, and he was wounded. Somebody patched him up and gave him a mount. I'm not curious about who it was. In fact, I'd rather not know. But after what happened at Parley Scott's, the man who befriends Steve, or any of his gang, won't be making things tough only for himself but for all of us."

He knew more than he cared to say. He felt he had gone far enough however. This was the first time he had talked with Webb since Caney had brought in his band of sheep. He had but to mention it to change the trend of the conversation immediately. What Webb had to say about the sheep was strong and to the point.

"Caney shouldn't have done it," Harvey agreed. "We're all with you on that, Webb. Have you seen anything of the sheep?"

"No, and I don't want to! The first time I catch 'em on my range, I'll turn 'em back! The second time it occurs, I'll kill every last one I can fire a slug at!"

Webb seemed to be well informed as to where Shad had purchased his sheep and how he had got them to his ranch.

"He went up across the Utah line to Lost Wagon and bought 'em from Hausman. I reckon the dirty sneak figgered he might be stopped if some of us got wind of what he was doin', so he drives 'em in durin' the night!"

Harvey had never seen Webb Nichols so aroused. The longer they talked, the more venomous he grew.

"By grab, I never expected to see anythin' eye to eye with Ringe, but I'm with him when it comes to sheep!" Growling, he swung up into the saddle. "If Shad Caney wasn't the skunk I been sayin' he is for years, he'd never have done this!"

"It's a raw deal," said Harvey. "But you don't want to do anything foolish."

"Hunh!" Webb snorted. "I'll do whatever's required!"

Harvey finished his chores before he went to the house. His mother was cooking supper. She came from hardy stock, and though she was nearing sixty, hard work and years of struggling to make both ends meet had not soured her. What education Harvey had he had received from her.

"What was Webb Nichols so excited about?" she inquired. "Shad Caney's sheep?"

"The sheep and what was done with those rustlers."

Martha Hume had found life so stern that the lynching of the three men failed to disconcert her.

"It's too bad such things have to be; but it was bound to happen, Harvey. The pity is that those who are really to blame will never see it that way. I mean Virgil and all the others who gave men like Joe Salazar good reason to believe they had a free hand with their thieving."

She was far more concerned about the sheep.

"I've known Shad Caney for thirty years, and he's always been a vicious, vindictive man," she said. "The money he'll make out of grazing a small band of sheep won't amount to anything. All it will do will be to make trouble."

"Virgil says Webb will kill Shad over this." Harvey took a cooky from the jar and munched it thoughtfully. "I don't like to say it, Mom, but that's the way I see it too—unless Caney gets into trouble with Ringe first."

"I don't put much stock in that," his mother declared, as she began setting the table. "I don't believe that man is mad enough to risk a fight with John Ringe. As for Webb killing him, it could be the other way around as well as not. I wouldn't put it past Shad Caney to have planned from the start to use the sheep as a bait to draw Webb into a trap. Thank the Lord, you've got a level head on you, Harvey! Trying to get along with folks is better than hating them and settling your arguments with a gun. I could never stand losing you the way I lost your father!"

Frank Dufors and the undertaker drove past the house the next morning. They cut down the bodies of the rustlers and took them into Mescal, where they were buried at county expense. Dufors indulged in a lot of talk about bringing charges against certain parties and asking for warrants. But he made no arrests, and everyone knew there'd be none.

It was taken for granted that word of what had happened at the entrance to Cochinilla Wash had traveled to the far reaches of the Desolations and the Ledge. There were some who said certain hardy individuals like Steve Jennings, Utah Sims, and Slick Carroll would feel called on now to make a raid just to prove that the fate that had overtaken Mescalero Joe and his two companions could not deter them.

If so, Steve and the men he ran with seemed to be taking their time about it. Though the big outfits had almost finished the spring branding there were no reports of stock being driven off. Harvey rode down to White Pine and had a talk with Eph Adkins, the storekeeper. Eph's store was all there was of White Pine.

"I don't hear nuthin' special," Eph declared. "Roberts comes in now and then. I reckon he's watchin' the store. He's heard Steve and the rest of 'em sneak in here sometimes to buy a little grub. He's a sorta friendly cuss."

"I've never seen him," said Harvey.

"No? Wal, he's tall, gaunt, kinda youngish, and nice lookin', yuh might say. Yuh don't git much talk out of him, but he's got a pair of gray eyes that bore right into yuh."

It was Eph's unwritten rule never to wait on a customer till the talk had been exhausted. As a result, little happened in Magdalena Basin that failed to reach his ears. But he kept a system of checks and balances on his conversation and always insisted on getting a little more than he gave. He brought up the matter of Shad Caney's sheep and what was likely to come of it. He had his own opinion, which he kept to himself, and tried repeatedly, and without success, to draw out Harvey. He gave up in disgust, finally.

"If Webb is keepin' his lip buttoned it's all right with me," he grumbled. "I figgered yuh might have heard what he's goin' to do about it. Let's see yore list!" There were only three items on it.

"I kin fix yuh up with the flour and the nutmeg but I can't let yuh have the molasses. I got half a barrel of the dang stuff and it's fermented on me! Yore ma would fire it back if I sold it to yuh."

Harvey had driven over. He carried the sack of flour out to the wagon. Eph followed with the empty molasses jug and the nutmeg.

"Get in!" he urged. "I'll untie the hosses for yuh."

"Eph, you've been around a long time and

can size things up," Harvey remarked. "Is there any grounds for thinking we've seen the last of the rustling?"

"No! Of course we ain't seen the last of it! But Roberts has raised the ante, Harvey. That's the only reason things is quiet right now. The game appears to've got a little too steep fer some of the boys."

Chapter Seven

Makings of Disaster

Eudora had been at Willow Creek almost a month before an opportunity to go into town presented itself. At supper, on Friday evening, Webb told her he had seen Harvey Hume during the afternoon and the latter had mentioned that he was driving in the next morning, with some butter.

"I asked him if he'd mind takin' you in, and he said he'd be glad to. I'll have to git you over to his place right early."

Eudora thanked him. She was surprised to discover how exciting the prospect of going to Mescal could be.

"I wish I could go with you," Elly said longingly.

"Sometime, when I'm drivin' in, mebbe you can go," Webb told her. "Harvey said you could have breakfast with him and his mother, Miss Stoddard. I offered to come over and git you tomorrow night but he said that wouldn't be necessary."

"The Humes is nice people," Mrs. Nichols assured Eudora. "The way Harvey buckled down and put his shoulder to the wheel is a credit to him."

Eudora received a warm welcome from Martha Hume the following morning. Before breakfast was over, she found herself sharing Mrs. Nichols's high opinion of Harvey and his mother. The latter had insisted to Webb that Eudora stay there the night and that he could pick her up the following afternoon on his way back from Elder Whitman's.

"It'll be late by the time you and Harvey get back from town," she told Eudora. "It would have been foolish to make you go on to the Nicholses', when you can just as well stay with us. You've been here a month and haven't got around at all. We can have Sunday dinner together and be finished before they stop for you. It'll be a change if nothing else."

"But won't I be keeping you from church?" Eudora asked.

"No, we go when the spirit moves us," Mrs. Hume declared, philosophically. "I enjoy listening to a good sermon, but I never was one to believe in going to church just for the going."

Eudora enjoyed the long drive with Harvey. They were of an age and saw many things with the same eyes. "It's been good to hear someone laugh again," she said, as they neared Mescal. "A little laughter and good will might change things considerably in the basin."

"I can't think of a better way to end all this hatred and fear and suspicion," said Harvey. "But it'll take a long time. Seems like there's always something new cropping up—like Shad Caney bringing in sheep—to keep the pot boiling. It isn't hopeless though; I know I've got enough people thinking my way to keep us out of another war unless the big outfits go crazy. As for Caney, I don't see how what he's done can end in anything but a showdown with Webb."

"Nor I," Eudora agreed. "I'm sure it's just a matter of time. I can't say anything, but it makes my blood run cold to see young boys like Verne and Jeb Caney being dragged into it. I don't know what Jeb does after he leaves school in the afternoon, but Verne no sooner reaches home than he saddles a horse and goes out armed to patrol the east range. I say east; I think that's correct."

"It is if it's the range toward Caney's line." Harvey touched up the team with the whip. "It would be a mistake for you to say anything to Webb. I don't know how boys would fit into a situation like this, back where you come from, but out here they're expected to shoulder some responsibility when they get to be fourteen, fifteen. The trouble is that they're treated like men one time and children the next. I don't know whether I make myself clear or not; but I'm sure Webb Nichols doesn't intend for Verne to do his fighting."

"Of course he doesn't. But it's so easy for something to go wrong; a boy of Verne's years hasn't any judgment. I hear the children talking about the sheep, at school. I suppose they hear things at home. I've ignored it so far, but I can see it's making bad feeling."

"Against the Caney children, of course."

Eudora said yes. "I suppose you're acquainted with them."

"I know them," Harvey acknowledged. "They're wild as bobcats."

"I haven't found them so," she declared. "Little Cissy is the only one who's given me any trouble." Eudora smiled. "And not what you would think, at all. She's developed quite a crush on me."

"I can understand why she might." Harvey's tone was bantering. "What did Cissy do?"

"It was my fault," said Eudora. "Elly used to wait after school was dismissed so she could walk home with me. One afternoon I found Cissy waiting. She said she wanted to walk home with me too, though she lives in the other direction. I tried to explain that to her. She insisted, and I let her have her way that day; but I decided the diplomatic thing for me to do was to walk home by myself. What time this afternoon will you be calling for me, Harvey?"

"About three. Will that give you time enough?"

"More than enough. I've got a long list of things I want to take back with me. Just trifles. I can gather them together in an hour or two and have time for a good visit with Aunt Jude and Uncle Dan."

The Stoddards were surprised to see her.

"Does this mean you've given up the school?" Mrs. Stoddard inquired at once.

"No, Auntie, of course not! There are some things I want to get, and I wanted to see the two of you. I had a letter from you about a week ago. Did you get mine?"

"Sure we did!" Mr. Stoddard answered. "Got it promptly!" He glanced at his wife. "The mail service isn't as bad as it's painted."

Mrs. Stoddard knew the remark was meant for her. "I'm reserving judgment as to that!" she declared tartly. "There's some other things happening out in the basin that you can't gloss over, Dan'l. The lynching of those three men, Dora! I ain't saying they didn't get what they deserved; but when I heard about it, with you right out there in the midst of it, I couldn't sleep a wink!"

"Jude, why bring that up again?" Dan protested. "I told you Dora is out there teaching school; that's all. You were so afraid you wouldn't hear from her; and then you said she'd have trouble with the children. But you hear from her promptly and she says she's doing fine. Why do you worry yourself this way?"

"I can't help it!" the little woman exclaimed nervously. "It may be foolish of me, but that's the way I'm constituted. I'm not timid for myself. It's different with you, Dora; you're so young and kind of helpless. I dread to think what would happen to you if you had to face one of those outlaws."

"Shucks!" Dan Stoddard scoffed. "She wouldn't know a rustler if she saw one! I bet you find things so quiet at Willow Creek that you're bored stiff."

"I wouldn't say that, Uncle Dan," Eudora returned laughingly. "But I seem to get along all right."

Dan returned to the drugstore and Eudora and Mrs. Stoddard went over the list of things the former wanted to take back with her.

"I guess I better get the geranium slips and pot them before I start dinner," said Aunt Jude. "If I haven't got pots enough I can borrow some from Mrs. Woodmancy. I don't know what sort of pictures you want. There's a pile of magazines in the cellar, but they're mostly fashion books. Maybe you can find something. Dan'l has that big calendar he got from that Chicago drughouse last year still hanging up on the door. You know the one I mean, with the basketful of puppies in the picture? He'll let you have it. The little ones will like it; it's as cute as can be! I see you've got dried beans on your list. Do you mind telling me what you want the beans for, Dora?"

"I'm going to make some bean bags, Aunt Jude."

"Bean bags?"

"Yes, for the girls. The boys seem to have plenty to keep them busy at recess, but the girls just stand around. No one has ever bothered to teach them any games. The bags will cost only a few pennies," she added as she saw her aunt frown.

"I should think the school board would supply things like that," Mrs. Stoddard declared. But to find Eudora concerned with things as prosaic as bean bags had a reassuring effect on her and she melted to enthusiastic co-operation. She had some remnants, she said, that would do for the bags.

"You can cut them out, Dora, and I'll run them through the machine. It's nice having you home with us again even if it is only for a few hours."

The time passed so quickly that she and Eudora were still tying up bundles when Harvey arrived. Mrs. Stoddard asked about his mother and thanked him for bringing Eudora in.

"I don't drive in on Saturday very often," he said, "but whenever I do, I'll be glad to pick her up."

Harvey kept the team moving right along on the way home, and though it was late when they drove into the yard, they found Harvey's mother waiting up for them. She insisted on getting supper.

"You'll rest better if you have something to eat," she told Eudora. "You sleep just as late in the morning as you please."

Eudora slept so soundly that she failed to hear the Nicholses drive by at an early hour. When she opened her eyes it was after eight. The appetizing aroma of fresh coffee drifted into the bedroom. Mrs. Hume heard her moving about and called a cheery good morning and told her not to hurry.

There was a warm, comforting friendliness in this house that Eudora found in marked contrast to the stern, gloomy air that rested so heavily on Webb Nichols's home.

"The Humes haven't let hatred poison them, and Webb Nichols has," she mused. "That's the difference. The whole family is marked with it."

The morning sped by too quickly for her, and not because there was anything new or exciting to do. It was a blessed relief just to be able to relax mentally and escape the gloomy predictions and feelings of impending disaster that she found at the Nicholses' table. The simple Sunday dinner was excellent, and she relished every mouthful.

"I'm no such cook as your Aunt Jude," Mrs. Hume declared in response to Eudora's compliments. "Of course, she's got more to do with, being in town. But then, I always say it's what a person brings to the table, as much as what's on it, that makes a meal good or bad. I suppose you do miss not having fresh milk at the Nicholses'. With growing children in the family, there's no excuse for not having a milch cow. I'll have Harvey put a jug in the rig for you, when they stop by."

It was two o'clock before they saw the wagon coming. Webb drove up to the door.

"We took our time and visited a little after meetin'; we didn't want to hurry you," he explained.

"We finished half an hour ago," Mrs. Hume told him. "Dishes washed up and everything. Rheba, I'd ask you to come in for a minute, but I know you've got a dinner to cook and want to get home."

Elly was clamoring for Eudora to sit on the back seat with little Hagar and herself. "There's lots of room, Miss Stoddard."

"You put these packages under the seat first, then I'll sit with you," Eudora consented. When she was ready, Harvey helped her into the wagon.

"I'll put the jug of milk up in front," he told her.

Webb let the womenfolk converse and directed his attention to Harvey. "Ringe began shovin' cattle on that leased range, east of Caney's line, yesterday afternoon. Eph Adkins says they drove some more stuff through White Pine this mornin'. That means Ringe will be keepin' some of his crew down this way from now on."

Eudora was listening. She didn't understand the significance of what he was saying, but she could see that Harvey did.

"He's moving in a lot earlier than he did last year," the latter remarked. "We had snow enough to give the grass a good start this spring. I suppose he figures that by using that graze now he can save some of his high range above the Santa Bonita until later in the season."

Webb shook his head. "That ain't the reason! Ringe knows there's sheep in the basin. That's why he's movin' some of his men down here. He's goin' to make shore nothin' strays across his line."

"Can you blame him?" Harvey queried. "You're keeping your eyes open for the same purpose."

"I didn't say I was ag'in what Ringe is doin'!" Webb grumbled. "I'm just tellin' you things is comin' to a head, Harvey! Just wait till the grass begins to dry up a little and stock has to cover more ground to git feed! You'll see what I mean!"

To hear him going on in that pessimistic vein, seeing strife and disaster wherever he turned, brought back to Eudora the very thought that had crossed her mind that morning. Whether this latest of his gloomy predictions was justified or not concerned her less, at the moment than the feeling that Webb's mind was locked in a vise; that where the possibility of trouble lurked, he insisted on ferreting it out and refused to find anything else.

Despite Elly's chattering Eudora thought of little else on the way home. Somehow, it dampened the enthusiasm with which she had been looking forward to getting back to school on Monday. That evening, going over the things she had brought out from town, she was conscious of it. "It's foolish to be discouraged just because Mr. Nichols feels as he does," she admonished herself. "I have my own ideas and I'll fight for them as long as I have the school."

She was sitting on the floor, the pictures she had torn from the magazines she had found in the Stoddards' cellar strewn about her, as she trimmed the edges with a pair of scissors. The cabin door was open. Verne stood there, gazing at her with a rapt expression on his face. It never occurred to her that she wasn't alone until a faint scraping of boot leather attracted her attention. She looked up, startled.

"Why, Verne, I didn't know you were here!" she exclaimed, not attempting to dissemble her surprise. Never before had he come to the cabin in the evening. "You gave me a start. Is there something you want?" she asked, the intentness of his gaze giving her a vague feeling of alarm.

From her position on the floor, he was a towering figure on the doorway, the yellow lamplight casting shadows that made his heavy features and neck muscles stand out in bold relief. Seen that way, he looked like anything but an adolescent boy.

"I—just wanted to tell you I'd be glad to carry some things to school for you in the morning," he said. His manner was awkward and self-conscious, but his boots did not climb over each other as they usually did whenever he spoke to her.

Eudora got to her feet. She had taken down her hair and tied it in back. It gave her a schoolgirlish look. "That's thoughtful of you, Verne," she told him. "You could carry the plants. I'll put them in a basket for you in the morning. Is there something else?" she questioned, when he did not start to leave, as she expected.

Panic began to grip the boy as she waited for him to answer. He was ready to turn and run, but something held him chained where he stood. "Yo're awful pretty with yore hair like that," he blurted out, hardly knowing what he was saying. "I'd do anything for you. If anybody ever tries to make any trouble for you, I'll kill him!"

Eudora's knees suddenly felt numb. In shocked amazement she stared at him. "You'll have to go, Verne!" she cried sternly. "I refuse to listen to another word from you!"

He sucked in his breath, raspingly. "Does that mean you like Jeb Caney better'n you do me?"

So that's the reason for all this! Eudora thought, a cold flood of understanding sweeping through her. "The two of you are just children to me!" she declared indignantly. "As for liking one of you better than the other, I've never given it a thought! And I don't propose to! I regard you and Jeb exactly as I do the other pupils!"

She pushed him out and closed the door. Turning out the light, she watched from the window and saw Verne crossing the yard. She was so angry and shaken that she couldn't reduce her racing thoughts to ordered thinking.

The absurd, stupid infatuation of an overgrown boy! she mused bitterly, as she undressed in the dark. *I suppose I should regard it as amusing, and let it go at that!*

It was not to be dismissed so lightly, however, for she realized it had its somber side and could easily turn into tragedy.

It kept her awake half the night. In the morning, she saw it in a somewhat different light, even to holding herself partly to blame. *It's just as Harvey said,* she thought. *You can't treat Verne as a man part of the time and expect him to consider himself a boy. I'll go out of my way to show him I regard him as a child, and that will end this nonsense!*

Chapter Eight

The Stock-Detective

School started off well enough on Monday, and as Eudora saw the enthusiasm with which the younger children greeted the pictures, flowers, and the bean bags, she felt fully repaid for her effort.

Verne and Jeb were interested, but they acted bored and indifferent, in order to impress Elly and the others with the fact that they were too old for such things.

Eudora ignored them. During the noon recess, she went out into the yard, and when Elly and Cissy had chosen sides, she showed them how to play One-I-Touch with the bean bags. She had the feeling that Verne and Jeb watched every move she made.

The two boys had words about something, just before they went back to their seats, and almost came to blows. Eudora ordered them inside.

They spent the afternoon glaring at each other until she sent Jeb to the blackboard to do a problem. His sharp features and piercing black eyes suggested that he had a certain keenness of mind. It was borne out by the ease with which he got his lessons, though he never seriously applied himself. As usual, he worked out the problem without any difficulty and returned to his seat. Verne took his turn at the blackboard. Arithmetic not only confused him, but whenever he had to stand up in front of the other pupils, his wits seemed to desert him. When he blundered for the third time, the children tittered.

Beside himself, he whirled around and caught the contemptuous grin on Jeb Caney's face. The blackboard eraser was the only missile within reach. He snatched it up and hurled it at Jeb. His aim was poor and the eraser thudded harmlessly against the wall.

The room was thrown into a turmoil. Eudora rapped for order, and in the charged silence that followed, she commanded Verne to pick up the eraser. He obeyed sullenly and came to the desk, as she requested.

"Verne, I'm going to ask you to apologize to all of us for your unspeakable conduct." Eudora was so furious her cheeks were bloodless.

He wasn't in any hurry to say he was sorry, but he finally got it out.

"And now," she said, "I'm going to send you home. Gather up your books. You can explain to your father why you were dismissed."

Verne said nothing; but his face paled at

thought of having to face his father. Without even a glance at Elly and his brother Moroni, he stamped out of the schoolroom and turned up the road for home. Hating Jeb with a devotion so intense that it had been warping his mind ever since early childhood, he held him to blame for his present difficulty. With such a spark to inflame him, he quickly whipped himself into a blinding rage, and when he was out of sight of the school, he left the road and turned back through the brush. Believing he was unobserved, he reached a spot where Jeb would have to pass on his way home. There, he waited. He was beyond caring about what Eudora might think, or any punishment from his father. His mind held room for only one thought: he'd beat the life out of Jeb Caney.

Eudora dismissed school at half-past three. Josie Hume's mother was waiting to drive her home. Elly and Moroni hurried off. The children who lived to the east walked down the road with the Caneys.

For once, Eudora was honestly glad to see them go, so that she might be alone. The flowers in the windows and the pictures on the walls mocked her as she went back to her desk.

"Ill stick to my guns!" she thought aloud. "If this had happened the first week or two I was here, I wouldn't have known what to do!"

She didn't know what Webb would have to

say about her sending Verne home. She told herself she didn't care. She slammed a book down on the desk angrily.

"He was careful to remind me that my business was to teach school!" she recalled. "Well, I'll let him know I'm making it my business! Verne Nichols won't be permitted to come back until his father guarantees me there won't be another incident like this!"

She was gathering up some papers to take home, when the excited voice of Cissy Caney reached her. She ran to the window and saw Cissy running toward the school. She hurried out to meet her.

"Miss Stoddard, you come, please!" Cissy cried. "Verne is killing Jeb! They're fighting something awful!"

Eudora ran back with her. She could see half a dozen children gathered in the road. Verne had Jeb on the ground and was punishing him viciously. A few feet away, a tall man sat on his horse, watching the fight and making no effort to stop it.

"Cissy, who is that man?" Eudora gasped indignantly.

"That's Clay Roberts, the detective!"

Fine business, enjoying the sight of two boys fighting! was Eudora's angry thought. *It's what you might expect from such a man!*

Jeb broke away from Verne and ran across

the road and reached under a discarded wagon box that had lain there so long it was falling to pieces. Verne started to follow him, but Clay left his saddle and pushed him back. To Jeb, he said, "You won't find what you're looking for; I've got your rifle on my saddle."

"You give it to me!" Jeb screamed.

"I'll give you nothing," Clay said flatly. "You head for home, now. I'll ride over to your place. You'll find me there when you show up. Go on!"

Eudora winced at sight of Jeb's battered and bloody face. She turned on Verne accusingly. "So this is the way you obey me, is it? I sent you home to speak to your father. Don't attempt to give me an excuse! I don't want to hear a word out of you! Just start walking. And the rest of you go too!"

The children began moving away. Eudora gave Clay a withering glance. "Why didn't you stop them? Were you enjoying it?"

He shook his head. "I don't like to see boys fighting any better than you do. But they all fight, and I know it's often the best way for them to let off steam."

This tall, softly spoken man, with the gray eyes was not at all as Eudora had pictured him. Though she prided herself on her ability to read faces, she searched in vain for any sign of hardness in him. He had a wide, generous mouth and the strong, determined chin she admired in a man.

"You're Miss Stoddard, of course," he said.

Eudora nodded. "How did you know Jeb had brought his rifle to school and left it in that old wagon box?"

"I watched him this morning. I was waiting for him when that Nichols kid jumped him. If young Caney had got his hands on his gun, he would have used it."

"I don't believe there's any question about that," she admitted. "What were they fighting about—the sheep?"

"No, something that happened at school. It didn't seem to be of any consequence. I suppose you've heard that the Diamond R has been putting stock on its leased range, east of here, for a couple days."

Eudora signified that she had.

"Somebody tried to beef a steer yesterday," he continued. "Whoever it was used a small caliber rifle, so it didn't amount to anything. One of Ringe's punchers saw this Caney boy out hunting later in the day. It seemed to add up to something. You can understand why I was interested when I saw him lugging his gun to school this morning."

She appreciated the seriousness of the incident and did not try to pretend otherwise. "Did you question Jeb?"

104

"No, I wanted to catch him actually firing a shot. He had a cow lined up in his sights, and then, for some reason, he changed his mind. I imagine he saw me."

"His brother and sister were with him?" she asked.

"He was alone. After he passed, I followed him. I figured he'd hardly take the gun into the schoolroom. I spent three or four hours trying to find where he had cached it before I located it under this wagon box. It's a twenty-five-twenty, which matches the slug that was dug out of that steer's hide yesterday."

Eudora gazed at him, so confident and unworried.

"You're very likely to have trouble with Jeb's father over this," she warned.

"I expect that's true," Clay replied. "But I've never known trouble to get better by walking away from it. I don't want to keep you standing here in the road, Miss Stoddard. May I walk back to the school with you?"

Eudora said yes, when she felt her answer should have been no. She had recovered her poise and in the process, somehow, her preconceived opinion about Clay Roberts had undergone a remarkable change. She had expected to find him a range rowdy in typical faded overalls and sweat-stained sombrero, picturesque enough on horseback but just a shuffling, bowlegged figure, once he had his feet on the ground; or, missing that, a sinister, hawk-nosed individual, with a brace of guns strapped around his middle. He was neither one nor the other. There was something in his quiet, reserved manner to suggest that he would measure up to any situation he encountered. He had a pleasant smile that lifted the corners of his mouth and warmed the gray eyes that some men found so fearsome. Indeed, Eudora found something indescribably appealing about him. But there was his reputation as a killer and that grisly business at Little Cochinilla Wash to give her pause. And yet, irrelevantly, she was glad she happened to be wearing one of her newest and most becoming dresses that set off her young figure to advantage.

Walking along at her side, leading his horse, his conversation contained no reference to the business that had brought him to Arizona. He said he understood she was from the East. His folks had come from Kentucky, he told her. He had gone back once for several months.

"I'd seen too much of this sagebrush country to get along without it," he remarked. "It gets into your blood. I've seen better grazing country than this, but there's something about it that hits me pretty hard."

"You haven't been spending much time in the basin, I understand," Eudora observed. "Does your being down here have any significance?" She was thinking of what Webb had said about matters coming to a head.

"Not particularly," he answered lightly. "That is, if you're referring to the sheep Caney has brought in. They're not my concern; my job is to curb the rustling. I don't know what Caney had in mind, but I think it was largely a bluff. Ringe has called it, and that'll very likely be the end of it. You're living at the Nichols place, I believe."

Eudora said yes.

"Caney may make some trouble for him over his sheep, but I don't think it will go beyond that. From what I hear, he stands pretty much alone. It was the feeling of some members of the Association that any attempt to stop the rustling would bring on a general showdown with everyone in the basin. The danger of that seems to have passed. Some of these small outfits are owned by men with cool heads. Harvey and Virgil Hume, to name a couple. All they ask is a fair deal, and that's what they're going to get if I can manage it."

"That's generous and honorable—if you mean it," said Eudora. "I've heard you described as a ruthless killer who whipped people into line with his guns. I must say you don't sound very much like one."

Clay smiled, finding her frankness refreshing.

"That's my reputation," he acknowledged, turning sober. "It's proven very valuable to me in my business. But I hope you'll reserve judgment on me, Miss Stoddard."

Eudora frowned. "Are you suggesting that you weren't responsible for the lynching of those three men at Cochinilla Wash?"

"I had no part in it, but it had my full approval," Clay replied, his mouth tightening grimly. "They got what they richly deserved. It's too bad such things have to be, but you mustn't see it with Eastern eyes, Miss Stoddard. This is a stockman's country. What little law there is either can't or won't, do anything to stop the thieving. These small outfits, down here in the basin, would feel the same way John Ringe and the other big owners do if it were their stock that was being run off."

"I'm afraid you don't make out a very good case for yourself," she said firmly. "There are worse crimes than rustling. If a man robs a bank, or stops a train, he is sent to prison; he isn't hanged for it."

Clay shook his head. "You miss the point, Miss Stoddard. There may be worse crimes than rustling, but if a bank is hoisted, it doesn't fold up; a railroad company doesn't go out of business because one of its trains is stuck up. But if you've got cattle running free on open range, you can't survive against organized rustling. You put your mark on your cows but the brand has never been invented that even a fair-to-middling rustler can't alter or obliterate with a running iron. He doesn't have to be an expert like Steve Jennings."

Eudora felt her throat tighten. "You speak as though you knew him—or is it just from hearsay?" she inquired, averting her eyes.

"I knew Steve before he turned to rustling—and afterward. He's smarter than most rustlers; he knows when it's time to move on. I hope he takes the hint this time. Funny, how little it takes to send a man down one road when he could just as well have taken another," he said reflectively, as old memories stirred in him. "But that's life, I guess. I understand Steve has some friends down this way. Did you ever see him?"

Somehow, Eudora felt the question wasn't as innocent as it sounded. "I'm not sure," she replied, with a counterfeit disinterest. "Strangers pass the school."

She was sure he was studying her carefully.

"Steve would hardly be stopping at the school to pass the time of day," he said lightly. "He knows he's playing a dangerous game and what the price will be if he stubs his toe. I imagine he won't complain about that part of it. Very few of them do, Miss Stoddard. They haven't any defense for what they do, and they know it. How does the old song go:

It was once in the saddle I used to go
   dancing,
It was once in the saddle I used to go gay;
First took to drinking, then to card playing.
Got shot for rustling; I'm dying today—

He paused, his eyes on Eudora. She was looking straight ahead, her lips tightly pressed together.

Take me to boot-hill and throw the sod
   o'er me.
I'm only a cowboy; I know I done wrong.

"That says it better than I can, Miss Stoddard. I hate to see you distressing yourself over Steve Jennings," he added, a deep and sympathetic understanding in his tone. "He isn't worth it."

"I'm not distressing myself, as you put it, nor trying to defend him," she insisted, her voice tense and brittle. "It's—just that I pity him."

Clay nodded without comment. His silence was more accusing than words. When they reached the gate, she faced him suddenly, the tautness of her face betraying her agitation.

"You knew I was lying when I said I wasn't sure if I had seen him."

"I'll have to say I thought you were," he

acknowledged. "It happened before I arrived in Mescal but I heard all the details from Cleve Johnson and the two boys who were with him when he talked to you. Naturally, I wondered how Steve had managed to slip through their fingers. The only way I could explain it was that you had locked him up inside the schoolhouse."

"What else could I have done?" she demanded boldly. "He was wounded; he couldn't use his right arm. He could have compelled me to hide him; he was desperate and I was here alone, helpless."

She told him how she had first seen Jennings at the window and what had passed between them.

"If I acted the way I did it wasn't because I'm opposed to Mr. Ringe and the interests you represent," she said, in conclusion.

"I'm sure of that," Clay assured her. "I've never expressed an opinion one way or the other about it to anyone. There's no reason why I should. I haven't any fault to find with what you did; if I had been placed as you were, I might have played it that way too."

Eudora gazed at him incredulously. "I hadn't expected to hear you say that. I'm green; I know very little about your Western ways. But I'm not so innocent, Mr. Roberts, as to think there can be any compromise between you and such men as Jennings. It's your job to hunt them down. Their answer will be to kill you whenever they get the opportunity. And yet, you don't seem to have any feeling about it. It's hard for me to understand."

"My quarrel with them isn't personal," Clay said. "They happen to be on one side of the fence and I'm on the other. As for the rest of it, I prefer not to think about it. I know my luck may run out on me some day. It's the chance I've got to take." His momentary seriousness faded. "I won't keep you any longer," he told her. "I'd appreciate it if you'd permit me to stop by again some other afternoon."

"Of course—if you happen to be passing," Eudora said casually, not wanting him to suspect her eagerness to see him again. "I hope you won't have any great difficulty with Mr. Caney. He's a violent-tempered man."

"So I understand," Clay remarked lightly. He swung up into the saddle with effortless grace. "Do you ride at all, Miss Stoddard?"

"No, I'm a real tenderfoot."

"You wouldn't have any trouble with a gentle horse. It's beautiful up on the Ledge, riding through the timber. I hope we can arrange it sometime—if you think you'd enjoy it."

"I'm sure I would," she murmured with complete honesty.

Something ran between them as they stood

there, and her eyes were suddenly warm and appealing. Clay nodded silently, and lifting his hat in farewell, rode away, tall and straight.

Eudora hurried inside, her heart singing. When she glanced up the road, he was just a bobbing figure in the distance.

Somehow, the school, her difficulties with Verne and Jeb, Webb's dire predictions and the ever-present threat of conflict of one sort or another no longer seemed as important as they had. When she started home, her step was light and there was a smile on her lips.

I hope he won't stay away too long, she mused. *It's no great distance from the Santa Bonita to Willow Creek.*

Chapter Nine

Plain Poison

Roberts rode into the Caney yard several minutes after Jeb reached home with Cissy and young Lorenzo. Shad and his wife had rushed out of the house and were standing a few feet from the kitchen door, with the children gathered around them. Jeb's battered face, and the tale he had told had thrown Shad into a convulsive rage. When he saw Clay coming, he slammed Lorenzo and Cissy out of the way and darted into the kitchen. He popped out a minute later, clutching his rifle.

"Hand over the boy's gun, and you turn around then and git outa here!" he roared.

Clay pulled up and regarded him calmly.

"You better hear what I have to say," he advised. "It may save you some trouble. Your boy put up a good fight; but he got licked, which isn't to his discredit; that Nichols kid is too big for him."

"Jeb would've settled his hash if you'd kept out of it!" Shad raged. "Why in hell did you have to stick yore nose in?"

"I didn't till this lad of yours knew he was

114

beaten and ran for his rifle. Fortunately, I'd picked it up quite some time before the fight started. You seem to be boiling over because I didn't give him a chance to use his gun. That's your business, Caney, but he's pretty young to be turning killer."

"I ain't interested in yore opinions!" Shad half raised his rifle. His rocky face was cruel and murderous. "Yank his rifle out of yore saddle boot and pass it over to him, as I told you!"

"I'll get around to that after I've had my say," Clay returned, watching him closely. "You're making a mistake to threaten me. I don't scare easily, for one thing; and for another, I'm wearing a forty-four in a shoulder holster and I'm reasonably fast with it. Don't make me reach for it, Caney; I never bluff with a gun."

Though Shad was beside himself in his black rage, the warning was not wasted on him. "Wag yore jaw and git done with it!" he snarled, lowering his gun a few inches.

Clay nodded. "It won't take me long. I don't know whether this boy acted with your knowledge or not, but he tried to beef one of Ringe's steers yesterday. He was all set to have a second try this morning, when he changed his mind. I was watching him. I figure he saw me."

"That's a lie!" Shad burst out viciously. "If he's out shootin' rabbits and one of Ringe's

115

critters gits in the way, that ain't the boy's fault!"

"It'll be your fault if it happens again." Clay's tone was hard and flat. "Bushwhacking stock is a game both sides can play. You'll find it expensive. That's all I have to say."

He pulled Jeb's rifle out from under his leg and tossed it to the boy.

"High and mighty, ain't you?" Shad's eyes blazed their hatred. "Yo're beginnin' to show yore hand, Roberts, ridin' in here and tryin' to push me around! Some of the damned idiots who've been listenin' to the Humes will begin to git their eyes open, now that you've let the cat out of the bag!"

Clay considered it an empty threat and was singularly undisturbed.

"Go ahead if you think this is the opportunity you've been waiting for to work up some feeling against me," he invited. "Maybe Frank Dufors will be interested. I understand he runs me down, behind my back, whenever he can get anyone to listen. I don't believe you'll have any luck in other directions; you cut your own throat when you turned sheepman."

"It's my business if I want to run sheep!"

"Sure!" Clay agreed. "But it's your funeral, not mine, Caney."

He swung his horse and rode away without a backward glance, though he realized that Shad might find the temptation to pick him off

116

too strong to resist. Experience had taught him, however, that in such circumstances a bold front was the best insurance.

The half-expected blast did not come, and in a few minutes he was out of range.

He'd be dangerous if he had any backing, he thought, his mouth losing its tightness.

There wasn't any question in Clay's mind but what Jeb had been acting on his father's instructions when he tried to kill one of Big John's steers. The purpose of it wasn't difficult to understand. Usually, in such cases, there was immediate reprisal by the injured party. Obviously, he felt, that was what Shad had counted on, even though it meant seeing the Diamond R crew sweeping across his line and destroying some of his stock. He could move his cows out of danger and let the sheep take it. Sheep were sheep, and though a score were slaughtered, he would have created a situation that could be exploited.

"His story would have been that the boy shot the steer by accident," Clay said to himself. "I don't know how far he'd have got with it but it's just as well Ringe let me handle it my way."

The scheme had misfired so badly that he refused to believe Caney would have another try at it. He was of an entirely different opinion regarding Jeb's quarrel with Verne Nichols.

"That trouble is a long way from being ended," he predicted. "With the encouragement they'll get at home those kids will be sure to go at each other again, and it may not be with their fists."

He had heard enough about the Caney-Nichols feud to convince him it would reach a bloody finale some day. The little he had seen of Verne and Jeb was more than enough to prove they had inherited all of its partisan hatred and were anxious to demonstrate how well they had learned their lesson.

For Webb Nichols and Shad Caney to feed youngsters of that age into their bitter, unreasoning feud was as reprehensible in Clay's eyes as in Eudora's. He realized there was little or nothing he could do about it; that it was not his concern. And yet, on her account, he was concerned.

Those brats will make trouble for her, was his sober thought. *She'll never be able to hold them in line, no matter what she does.*

He knew she'd try; that she had courage and a mind of her own. The course she had taken when Steve Jennings walked in on her was proof enough of that.

A smile played over Clay's mouth as he imagined her surprise when she discovered the identity of her visitor. To have her confirm his surmise that she had helped Steve to elude capture meant little to him. He knew John Ringe wouldn't feel that way if he ever learned about it. Undoubtedly, Eudora would lose the school; Big John had suffered too many losses at Jennings's hands to be satisfied with anything less.

Roberts put the thought away from him; Ringe would never hear anything from his lips. Heading up the basin for the Diamond R and the Santa Bonita, he indulged in some pleasant daydreaming. He had been many places and known many women but had always remained fancy-free. The prospect of settling down somewhere and trading the freedom of his foot-loose existence for the responsibilities of a family man had never appealed to him. He had many reasons for feeling as he did; the dangerous nature of his calling was always a handy and potent argument. But in some obscure way the music of Eudora's voice and the magic in her blue eyes had put them in retreat.

"She's different," he admitted. "I don't know what a man could look for in a woman that he wouldn't find in her. But I've been a fiddle-foot too long to think of turning serious now; if I ever get around to hanging up my hat and calling some place home, it won't be Magdalena Basin."

Though he knew how to assert himself when occasion demanded, he was essentially a humble man, and not for a moment did he consider himself a great catch.

Not for her nor for anyone else, for that matter, was his disparaging thought. *She hasn't been waiting for me to come along and charm her. Someone from Ohio will be showing up in Mescal one of these days and will carry her off. The sooner I put her out of my mind, the better.*

That attitude was not reflected in his resolve to arrange his riding so that he might see Eudora again soon. Some afternoon, after school had been dismissed, he'd drop in on her and pretend he just happened to be in the neighborhood on business; he didn't want her to get the idea he was running after her.

The days were getting long; the sagebrush was losing its greenish spring tinge. Now, wherever a rider moved over the road, his horse kicked up a telltale cloud of dust. It reminded Clay that May was slipping away.

He had the sun at his back all the way to the Santa Bonita. Several times he saw little moving balls of dust that indicated horsemen, moving in the direction of the Diamond R. He thought nothing of it until he noticed several more. The speed at which they traveled suddenly began to interest him. He considered it unlikely that any of Big John's riders would be pushing their broncs in that fashion, after a hard day's work. Coconino Williams, Pat Redman, and other cowmen often rode over to see Ringe in the early evening, but they hardly would be in such haste unless something were amiss. The thought was enough to prompt him to use the spurs.

When he rode into the yard, he found half a dozen horses tethered at the rail outside Ringe's office. He recognized old Coconino's gray dun and Pat Redman's favorite claybank gelding. Before he could swing down, Big John stepped out on the gallery and beckoned to him urgently.

In addition to Coconino and Redman, Clay found Ed Stack and his foreman, Cape Longyear, and two other members of Association gathered in the office with Big John. A glance at their faces told him there was something decidedly wrong. An angry outburst from Stark greeted him.

"You've been busy on the wrong side of the basin, Roberts! Jennings got into me sometime today, and good! Do you know what we call the Painted Meadows?"

"Yes—"

"That's where he hit me! Cape, here, rode up there this afternoon and had a look around!"

"I don't know how much they got away with," Longyear spoke up. "Fifty, sixty head, at least."

"And all graded stuff!" Stack stormed. "We're paying you a fancy figure for your services, and this is what I get!" He glared around the office at the others. "I went along with you against my better judgment in hiring this man! I told you hiring a stock-detective wouldn't help us a bit!"

"Yeh, you didn't want to do nuthin', Ed," old Coconino reminded him caustically. "You was all for meetin' the nesters halfway and lettin' the rustlin' take care of itself. Seems that when you git burned yo're as warlike as the rest of us."

"What makes you so sure it was Jennings?" Clay asked Stack.

"He left a message for me! I've got a corral up there. He burned it on the corral gate: *Thanks, S.J.;* that's what it says! The dirty skunk took the time to heat a running iron; that's how sure he was of himself!"

"I never heard of him havin' more'n three or four men in his gang," said Longyear. "He had more'n that with him today. Judgin' by the hosstracks, I'd say six, mebbe seven."

"Did you pick up their trail?" Clay inquired, sober but unexcited.

"Shore! I didn't follow it no distance; I figgered it was up to me to git back to the house. It was yore idea that if anybody got touched up that word was to be spread in a hurry so we could block off the Wash and the short cuts up to the Ledge."

"That's been attended to," Big John told Clay. "Between us, we've sent a dozen men up there. Jennings won't find it easy to get through anywhere from the hot springs down to the Red Cliffs."

"Which way was he heading?" Clay asked Stack's foreman.

"In the general direction of the Red Cliffs."

Clay found a chair and sat down. "This may not be as bad as it seems," he declared quietly. "When Steve finds he can't get through, he'll swing around the cliffs and come up on the eastern slope of the Desolations."

"There won't be nuthin' else he can do!" Coconino attested stoutly. "He can drift one hell of a ways down through the bluffs; but the river will turn him back in the end! He can't git acrost the Colorado!"

"And that's tough country for cattle," Pat Redman observed. "No water."

"I know all that!" Stack countered. "Jennings is no fool! What's to stop him from swinging west and heading for the Nevada line?"

"The best reason in the world," Clay answered. "The market for rustled steers doesn't lie in that direction. Your cows aren't worth anything to Steve unless he can turn them into cash. That means the San Juan country, over in Utah. It's as simple as that."

There was a nodding of heads around the office. It further infuriated Stack. He leveled his eyes on Roberts. "I want something more than talk from you; I'm helping to foot the Association's bills! I want to know what you propose to do!"

"I'm going after Steve. That's my job. I didn't think there was any question about it."

"Of course not!" Big John growled, out of patience with Stack. "You don't intend going alone, Clay?"

"No, I'll take Cleve Johnson with me if you're agreeable to it."

"Certainly," Ringe said. "He knows those wastelands better'n most of us."

"It may take me a day or two to locate that bunch," Clay continued. "I'll send Cleve back as soon as I do. He'll tell you where to find me. When you come, come strong; and carry grub and water with you so you can stay out a few days. In the meantime, sit tight and give me a chance," he continued, speaking particularly to Stack. "I never gave the Association any reason to understand if it hired me there'd be no more rustling. If you want to call things off, this is the time to say so."

"We're satisfied a hundred percent with what you've done!" old Coconino whipped out. "I don't blame you fer gittin' up on yore ear, havin' to listen to the line of talk Ed's been givin' you. What in hell's wrong with you, Ed? You ain't lost those critters yet; and if you do, it won't be the first time Jennings has had you over a barrel! What'd you expect Roberts to do, camp up there in the Painted Meadows?"

The approving response it drew from Big John and the others took some of the belligerence out of Stack. "I'm sorry if I blew up a little," he muttered. "I only hope Roberts and the rest of you are right about Jennings driving up the eastern slope of the Desolations when he finds the way blocked on this side. If you are, maybe there's a chance of getting my stock back. But it won't be as easy as some of you seem to think; Jennings has got a tough bunch riding with him. They'll put up one hell of a fight if we get them cornered. How soon are you goin' to pull away, Roberts?"

"I'll give myself half an hour," Clay told him, getting to his feet. "I'll look up Cleve and start getting organized, unless someone's got something more to say."

"Better have your supper before you pull out," Ringe advised. "I'll take care of things at this end. We'll be ready to ride as soon as we hear from you."

The meeting broke up and Coconino and the others rode home. Big John found Clay and

Cleve Johnson in the dining-room. He sat down with them.

"Did you find out anything in the basin?" he asked.

"It was that Caney kid, John—the big one. I had it out with him and his old man. Caney's as dangerous as a rattler, but I don't believe you'll have any more trouble with him for the present."

As he ate, he gave Ringe an account of what had occurred. The big man expressed his satisfaction.

"He had the trap baited for us all right. I'm glad he knows we're wise to his game. I figure Shad is smart enough to know he won't have a leg to stand on if he starts beefing my cows now."

The quarrel between Verne and Jeb was of little consequence to John Ringe. Clay was unwilling to have it that way. "You're a member of the school board; you'll have to share part of the responsibility for whatever happens there," he declared pointedly.

Big John straightened up, puzzled. "Good Lord, what do you think is going to happen, that you talk that way? Another fight between those boys? They've been fighting for years."

"Did a gun ever figure in their arguments?"

"I don't know that it did—"

"Well, that was the case this afternoon. That

Nichols kid knows Caney would have killed him but for me. The idea will grow on him that he better do something about it. If I've got the situation sized up correctly, those two young bucks will be throwing lead at each other one of these afternoons."

"And what would you have me do about it?" The big man leaned back in his chair and shook his head disgustedly. "I'm not responsible for what those boys do! They've been raised wrong! It's up to Shad Caney and Webb Nichols to keep them from going hog wild!"

"That's all true," Clay admitted. "I wasn't suggesting that you could do anything about the two boys. I'm more concerned about what may happen to the younger children and Miss Stoddard if those fools start a gun fight near the school. She'll try to stop it. You know the chance she'll be taking, walking into that sort of shooting."

"That's something I hadn't considered," the boss of the Santa Bonita acknowledged, forgetting his umbrage. "I don't want to expose her or the little ones to that sort of danger. The best thing to do would be to close the school for the rest of the term and send Miss Stoddard into Mescal. But, hell's fire! Neither Caney nor Nichols would ever agree to that. The only thing I can do is to urge the girl to go into town. Without a teacher, the school will have to close."

"She won't go, John. She'll consider it her duty to stick it out. You know her a lot better than I do, but I didn't have to talk to her five minutes to see she's got plenty of iron in her. There's something you can do though. It won't come easy to you."

"I'm listening," Ringe said cautiously.

"See Harvey Hume in the morning and ask him to keep an eye on her."

Big John rejected the suggestion with a violent shaking of his head. "I can't ask a favor of him!" he declared flatly.

"You can if you're big enough," Clay insisted. "You could afford to break the ice and meet him on even terms. It might prove to be the wisest move you ever made."

Ringe mulled it over soberly. "You're going to be away for a few days and so am I," he said, finally. "If I'm going to speak to anyone it will have to be Hume; there's no one else down there I'd even consider approaching. There's things about that youngster I admire. I've got to admit it."

Clay kept his eyes on his plate and smiled to himself. "What time tomorrow will you see him?"

"I'll make it early in the morning," was the gruff response. Ringe glanced across the table at Cleve. "Where are you heading for first?"

"The San Carlos Swell. They'll have to cross

it. Clay agrees that we couldn't find a better place to cut their trail."

Big John nodded. "I don't have to tell you boys to be careful. No matter how things break, I don't want you to attempt to close in on that bunch till help reaches you."

"We won't make that mistake," Clay assured him.

"Well, I hope not!" the big man growled. "Jennings will have his pals Utah Sims and Slick Carroll siding him, and they're just plain poison! I'll get out of here now so you can finish your supper. If we don't hear from you by tomorrow or the next day, we'll know you've run into trouble, and we'll start looking for you."

He was on the gallery steps when Clay and Cleve jogged out of the yard twenty minutes later. He raised his hand in a farewell salute.

"That advice he was givin' us was meant mostly for me," Cleve remarked, with a grin. "The old man remembers that Jennings put a slug into me a couple of years ago that had me flat on my back for two months. Reckon he figures I might be a little overanxious about squarin' things."

"If you feel anything like that coming on, you want to change your mind about it," Clay said grimly. "It was good advice he gave us, and I'm following it whether he meant it for me or not."

Chapter Ten

The Fight at Skull Tanks

An hour before dawn Roberts and Cleve stood on the crest of the barren San Carlos Swell. They picketed their horses and curled up in their blankets until sunup.

Daylight revealed a world that bore no resemblance to Magdalena Basin. Here was no living green thing, not even dwarf sage. As far as the eye could see there was only sand and grotesquely carved sandstone peaks. Along the swell, the rimrock was decayed and tottering. It was a world that was old and lifeless. The wind had been at work here for centuries, eroding and sculpturing a fantastic land. To the south, it dropped away in a series of gigantic stairs toward the Colorado.

Clay gazed at it with narrowed eyes. In all that vast expanse, lost in the far distance in a blue haze, nothing moved. The dawn breeze was beginning to kick up little dust devils that danced in the thin, shimmering air.

"Looks tough, eh?" Cleve inquired, catching the expression on Clay's face. The latter nodded.

130

"Steve must know this country, to think he can run a bunch of cattle through it. A stranger wouldn't have a chance."

They ate a cold snack before they began moving along the swell. Half a hundred cows would kick up enough dust to pollute the air for some time after they passed. Clay caught Cleve sniffing the air for sign of it.

"No use, Cleve," he said. "They must be hours ahead of us."

They followed the swell for four miles or more. In such country as this it was impossible to move a herd without leaving a trail a child could follow. The sun was over an hour high when Clay found it.

"From what I see, Steve and his pals wasn't hazin' that stuff along very fast when they passed here," Cleve observed.

"No, taking their time all right," Clay agreed. "It could mean they know they've got a long piece to go without water and just letting the stock drift along is the only way to get it through."

They came down from the swell and followed the trail until noon. It was still heading south. It was evident to Clay by now that Jennings wasn't going to attempt to cross Hurricane Ledge.

"I guess the old fox figured I'd have it blocked off," he said. "The only reason he's dropping down this far is so he can swing wide around the Ledge and hit into the lower hills of the Desolations."

"I'd stake my life on it," Cleve declared. "He's goin' to be lookin' for water and he knows that's where he'll find it."

He got down from the saddle and drew a map in the sand. On it he traced the rustlers' course, as he saw it.

"You'll find some springs here," he said, making an indentation with his finger. "The only name I ever heard for them is Skull Tanks. It's noon now. By this time tomorrow Jennings will be showin' up there. Do you figure you can find the tanks?"

"Can you give me a landmark I can go by?"

"Sure! Hat Butte! It looks like one of those old stovepipe hats. You can't miss it. Stay to the north a mile or two. If I go now I can be on the Santa Bonita before midnight. The boss said he'd be ready to ride whenever I got in. If he is, we can join up with you just about noon tomorrow."

"All right," Clay told him. "Get started; we won't lose any time."

He turned east after they parted. Save for an occasional beady-eyed lizard, sunning itself on a rock outcropping, he saw no living thing through the afternoon. When evening came on, and he had the sun behind him, he caught his first glimpse of Hat Butte. Its outline was unmistakable.

His mind was free of anxiety as far as rustlers were concerned. He had every reason to believe Steve Jennings would find a surprise waiting for him at Skull Tanks that would prove his undoing.

If we snag him, my job here will be about finished, he mused.

It turned his thoughts to Eudora; when his job was done, he'd be moving on. The prospect, for some reason, was not pleasant to contemplate. He promised himself he would see her as soon as he got back to the ranch. It might be two or three days from now. She'd hardly know what was keeping him away. He could explain that to her; he didn't want her to think he'd forgotten her.

He slept that night in a sandy depression north of Hat Butte. In the morning he would have risked a fire and boiled some coffee had he been able to find anything that would burn.

Locating Skull Tanks was a simple matter, for even at a distance of half a mile he could see a fringe of green around a limestone outcropping. He had water in his canteen, so he did not go up the tanks. Several hundred yards north of them, a crumbling ridge rose above the plain. He placed his horse where it was not likely to be seen and climbed the ridge on foot. It gave him a view of the broken country to the south. From any one of half a dozen low ridges and tangled piles of malpais a man could safely reconnoiter Skull Tanks. He considered it a certainty that Steve would look things over carefully before he drove in.

The morning was still young but Clay asked himself what he would do if they appeared before help reached him. He had to admit it would be suicide, facing them alone, one man against seven. He shook his head over it.

That's borrowing trouble, was his scolding thought. *I've always found John Ringe as good as his word; he'll be here in time.*

But the morning wore away without bringing either friend or foe. As he lay stretched out on the ridge, the sun hot on the back of his neck, he asked himself repeatedly if anything could have happened to Cleve Johnson to prevent him from reaching the Santa Bonita. A horse could break a leg; even an experienced rider could be thrown. These and a dozen other possible mishaps occurred to him. The position of the sun told him it was noon.

"Nothing for me to do but sweat it out," he muttered grimly.

He stubbornly refused to believe he was waiting in the wrong place for Steve and his men; water they must have, and it would draw them to Skull Tanks as surely as a magnet attracts steel.

He scanned the horizon to the south for sight of a moving cloud of dust. Several times in the following thirty minutes he was sure he saw one. It hung in the air briefly and then disappeared. He realized the wind was stiff enough to account for that.

Scanning a ridge off to his right a quarter of a mile, he thought he saw something move. A few moments later a horseman stood outlined against the sky. The rider stood up in his stirrups and waved his arm in a signal for someone to come ahead. He rode down the far side of the ridge then. Ten minutes later Clay saw the bunched cattle moving toward him. He counted the men with them and they totaled seven.

"I'll have to let them come in," he decided. "If they spot me, I'll hold them off as long as I can; if they don't I'll let them water and then tag along after them."

The cows smelled the water and began to run. Suddenly, however, Jennings and his men whipped ahead of them and turned them back and sought the protection of a ridge.

Clay instantly surmised the reason. Ringe and his party were here at last! A few minutes later they swung into view—Ringe, Pat Redman, old Coconino, Ed Stack, their foremen, and several others including Cleve. A dozen in all. Clay went down to his horse and rode out to meet them.

"Thank God we got here in time!" Stack barked at him. "We'll make short work of that bunch of blacklegs!"

Clay glanced at Ringe and Coconino and was relieved to see they didn't share Stack's opinion that it was going to be an easy matter to finish off Steve and his bunch.

"We better talk things over before we try to close in," Coconino advised. "They can make a stand on that ridge. If we go at 'em head on, they're goin' to pick off some of us."

"What of it?" Stack rapped. "Didn't any of us figure this was going to be a tea party!" A slug from the ridge kicked up the dust a few feet in front of him. The spent slug ricocheted off a rock. He glared at it disdainfully. "There's nothing stopping us from dropping back to the west and getting on top of that ridge with them!"

Big John turned to Clay. "What do you suggest?"

"I'd swing around the ridge and try to take them from the rear."

"That's leavin' the door wide open for them to make a run for the mountains," Pat Redman objected. "I agree with Ed that we didn't make this ride to see them slip through our fingers. We can throw as much lead as they can. I'm for sailin' into 'em and wipin' out the whole damned bunch!"

The majority felt as he did.

"All right," Ringe accepted grudgingly. "I think it's a mistake, but since that's the way you want it, that's what we'll do. Spread out and keep the Tanks at your back. When we're in position, I'll raise my hand. That'll be the signal to charge."

He rode aside with Clay and told him he had seen Harvey. "He promised to watch things at the school. I'm glad I had the talk with him."

In the course of the next two hours they tried no less than five times to rush the ridge before even Stack was convinced the rustlers couldn't be dislodged by a frontal attack. Pat Redman was down with a bullet in his groin and seriously wounded; Cleve's right shoulder had been shattered; Bill Rowan, Coconino's foreman, his trigger finger shot away by a bullet that had struck his rifle and pinged off to bury itself into his chest, had dropped out of the fight.

Clay took off his hat and smiled grimly at the bullet hole just above the hatband, as they dropped back to Skull Tanks, out of range of the guns on the ridge. It had been close enough to clip his hair.

"We've had enough of this nonsense!" Big John growled. "We'll never flush them out this way! Roberts had things sized up correctly!"

"Shore he did!" old Coconino burst out fiercely. "That bunch will fight like wolves as long as we got 'em cut off! Git around in back of 'em and they may take a run! If they do, they'll turn them cows adrift!"

"That won't satisfy me, but it'll be something!" Stack muttered. "We better get Pat started for home; I reckon Bill and Cleve can get him in." They tied Redman in his saddle and Rowan and Cleve started off with him on the long ride back to the basin.

Attacking the rustlers from the rear was successful on the first try. With the way to the north and possible escape left open, they took it promptly for they had two men down, one of them Steve himself. They forgot all about Stack's cows and streaked for Skull Tanks. Ringe and his posse dashed after them, but the rustlers stood their ground and drove them back. The position of quarry and pursuer was now reversed.

Longyear and three others had been given the job of holding the cows. From the ridge, the others saw the rustlers water their broncs and quench their own thirst. They flattened down on the limestone outcropping then, and gave every indication of their intention to remain there. Old Coconino gazed at them with squinting eyes. "By grab, they're invitin' us to come ahead whenever we git ready, John!"

Ringe nodded. "The price will be high if we try it. The way they're settling down they intend to stick it out there till dark. If they can do that, you know what it means." He was speaking to all now. "They'll pull away before the moon gets up and shake us off during the night. We'll have had our trouble for nothing, or almost. Ed's recovered his stock; I suppose that counts for something."

"We've done better than that, John," Clay declared. "They've had two, maybe three, men wounded. One of them is Jennings. I was in close enough to be sure about that. He had to be helped down from the saddle. This raid doesn't show them any profit."

"You arguing against shooting it out with them?" Stack demanded with surly contempt.

"I think it would be worse than foolish!" Clay whipped back, his patience with Stack running out. "You had things your way this afternoon and we lost three men and accomplished nothing. If you want to make another mistake like that, go to it, but don't ask the rest of us to follow you."

"What would your idea be?" Stack challenged.

"Those cows are crazy for water. Instead of trying to hold them, I'd let them go. They know there's water ahead of them. They'll put their tails up and stampede into it. When Jennings sees them coming he'll realize they'll be climbing over his bunch in a few minutes. It won't leave him anything to do but pull out in a hurry."

"By Christopher, I ain't getting those steers back to see 'em shot down before my eyes!" Stack roared.

"Steers are cheaper than men!" Big John interjected. "I think Roberts has hit the nail on the head!"

"Sounds good to me!" Coconino joined in. "I don't know as there'll be any cows killed! When those gents out there see that bunch comin' at 'em, spooked up with thirst, they'll skedaddle! It'll be a stern chase for us, but we may be lucky enough to drop a couple of 'em!"

Stack continued to protest, only to be overruled. The cattle needed no persuasion to be put in motion. With their heads down and tails high, they broke around the end of the ridge and made a wild dash for Skull Tanks.

Steve and his men tried to turn them with a blast of gunfire. When that failed, they took to their horses and fanned out for the north.

Though they were hotly pursued, they managed to win across several miles of open country to the first fold of the lower foothills of the Desolations. The terrain was in their favor now, and they took advantage of it, making a brief stand whenever they had the enemy at a disadvantage, and then dropping back to the next likely looking ridge or rocky dike. They were fighting for time as much as anything else. The sun was getting low. Another hour, and they could well hope to fade away into the mountains.

They were firing from behind a shoulder-high ledge when Roberts, Coconino, and Charlie Petrie broke away from the others and swung around them. Caught on the flank, they retreated at once.

Clay saw a man topple out of the saddle as they fell back. A second rider turned and started to pick him up. A glance was enough for him, however, and he let him drop and scurried after his companions.

When Coconino came up to the dead man, he identified him as Chuck Beeson. "That ole sidewinder's been outside the law for twenty years! He's deader'n a mackerel!"

They left Beeson where he had fallen and pressed on. Stack greeted the news that Jennings had lost a man with vociferous satisfaction.

"I'd like to wipe out every one of 'em!" he rapped.

It was a hope that was not to be realized. A narrow canyon opened behind the rustlers. They made for it, and from its mouth were able to hold the posse at bay.

"It's no use," Ringe announced, as darkness

fell. "We've done all we can. It won't do us any good to hang on here; they'll be far away by morning."

It was sound advice, and Stack and the others accepted it. Weary, hungry, with a night's riding still ahead of them, they turned back to Skull Tanks to round up Stack's cows.

"What about Beeson?" Clay asked.

"Pile some rocks over him and let it go at that!" Coconino answered. "That's better'n he deserves!"

They were at Skull Tanks in an hour. They had food to satisfy their hunger and tobacco to take the edge off their weariness. Stack's cows had feasted on the grass around the tanks and had bedded down for the night. At first, they stubbornly refused to take the trail. Once they were moving along, however, they were handled without too much difficulty.

Clay dozed in his saddle for an hour. Ringe rode at his side, relaxed and half asleep. The penetrating chill of the high places knifed into their bones and jerked them awake.

"Cold," Clay muttered. "Must be late."

"After midnight," Big John informed him, glancing at his watch in the moonlight. "Still a long piece to go."

He filled his stubby pipe and puffed on it for a while.

"I must have been dreaming back there," he

said. "Something about Pat Redman. He was in pretty bad shape, Clay. I hope we don't lose him. Pat's a good man."

"They must have him on the way into Mescal by now," Clay replied. "Have you got a good doctor?"

"Yes, Deering is all right. He's got a couple rooms in his house that he uses for a hospital. He'll keep Pat there. Rowan and Cleve will need his attention too. The news will fly over the basin that there's been a big fight. Things went our way, but we could have done better."

"We did well enough," said Clay. "I think you'll have proof of that in the days to come. I don't know how seriously wounded Jennings is. I don't think it matters particularly. It's enough for me that we've proved to him and his gang that rustling around Magdalena Basin isn't profitable any more. That's what counts. It's been my experience that when you show rustlers their game doesn't pay, they move on to greener pastures. I'll be surprised if Steve makes another raid."

"You honestly mean that?" Ringe asked soberly.

"I do. I'm afraid the end of my job is almost in sight."

Chapter Eleven

Bushwhacked

Clay had expected to be gone three or four days, when he promised himself he would see Eudora as soon as he got back to the basin. Though it had not taken him that long, he saw no reason for staying away, and when she dismissed school that afternoon, he was at the gate.

Eudora had heard about the fight with the Jennings gang, during the day. She was relieved to see Clay back, unharmed; but with feminine perversity tried to conceal the fact. "I hadn't expected you so soon," she said. "When did you get back?"

"About daylight. I was going to pretend I just happened along this afternoon, but I'm not going to do it. I was worried about you and I might as well admit it."

Eudora gave him a smile that fully repaid him for his honesty. "It was thoughtful of you to ask Mr. Ringe to see Harvey on my account. It wasn't necessary; I've been perfectly safe. Will you come in?"

She led the way into the schoolhouse and sat

down at her desk. Clay pulled up a chair. As he sat there with his hat on his knee, Eudora saw the ominous looking bullet hole above the band. She reached out for the hat and Clay saw her cheeks pale.

"It was that close!" she exclaimed barely above a whisper.

"It was close," he acknowledged. "A miss is as good as a mile, they say."

At her insistence, he told her of what had taken place at Skull Tanks and the running fight that followed. It left her frightened and dejected.

"I suppose you've been through such things so often you take them as a matter of course," was her sober comment. "Has it ever occurred to you how selfish you are, taking such chances with your life? It might be precious to someone," she finished looking away.

"If you were that someone it would make a difference—a big difference," he said tensely, his heart in his eyes as he gazed at her fondly.

He reached out and caught her hand and she did not draw away.

"I've saved my money. I could hang up my guns without regret and turn to something safer, Eudora."

"That's something I haven't any right to ask," she murmured softly, the pulse in her cheek beating faster. Her eyes met his appealingly.

"Please don't make me say any more now, Clay!"

She withdrew her hand and they sat there without speaking for a long moment before she said, "I suppose you noticed that Verne and Jeb were not in school today."

Clay nodded. "Haven't they been back since they had their run-in the other afternoon?"

"No, and I'm afraid they won't be back. To my surprise Mr. Nichols supported me, but whcn hc hcard about Jeb and his rifle he was furious, of course. The upshot of it was that he said Verne was done with school. From what Cissy has to say, the Caneys feel the same way. I don't know whether it was done deliberately or not, but their sheep got across the line yesterday afternoon. Verne and his father drove them off."

"Well, I must say you take it calmly enough!" Clay exclaimed, straightening up, surprised. "It was one of the things I was afraid of for you. Were any shots fired?"

"No. The sheep were driven off but they weren't harmed."

"That'll follow, and quickly! There'll be shooting, and it may not be out on the range, either." Clay's voice was rough with conviction. "Eudora—I want you to promise me you'll start for the Humes at the first sound of gunfire and stay there until this trouble is over!"

"Certainly you don't think the Caneys would attack the house!" she protested.

"I don't know what they'll do," Clay declared sharply. "There's no reason why you should be caught in their quarrel."

Eudora found his concern for her precious.

"I'll go to the Humes if that will make you feel better," she said. "But you can't ask me to pick up and run without reason. If there is any shooting, chances are it will be finished before I learn anything about it."

"If that's the way it turns out, so much the better," he told her. "You will be careful?"

"I promise," she said lightly. "I'm going to let you walk home with me."

"I wondered if you'd permit me."

Eudora laughed, he was so sober about it.

"Permit you?" she echoed. "Why do you put it that way, Clay?"

"I imagine Webb Nichols won't relish seeing you in my company."

"I'm afraid it's a little late to keep him from knowing we're friends. Children are terrible gossips, Clay; by suppertime everyone will know you were calling on me this afternoon. As for Mr. Nichols, he's free to think whatever he pleases."

"You're under no obligation to him, Eudora?"

"No, and I want him to understand that I'm not."

When she had gathered up some papers she wanted to take home, she turned the key in the lock and they went down the road together, with Clay leading his horse. Just being in each other's company gave them a deep sense of excitement and happiness that found expression without resorting to words.

Verne was in the yard when they turned in. His eyes blazed with jealousy at seeing them together. With a hostile scowl darkening his face, he hurried off to the barn.

"There's a lot of wolf in that kid," Clay said tightly. "Do you have any trouble handling him?"

"Verne will do anything for me," she remarked with a vague note of uncertainty that he caught.

"Look out for him," he advised. "He's likely to misunderstand your being kind to him."

They talked for a minute at the cabin door.

"When will I be seeing you again, Clay?" she asked, as he was about to ride away.

"In a day or two. If you can arrange it, maybe we can ride up in the timber this week-end."

He raised his hat and was gone then. A few minutes later, Webb was at the door, a deep anger in his eyes.

"Miss Stoddard, I ain't presumin' to tell you how to pick yore friends, but I don't want Roberts snoopin' around here," he declared bluntly. "That's final, and it's all I have to say!"

Eudora faced him with rare courage and refused to be flustered. "I'm glad you recognize my right to choose my friends," she said evenly. "I recognize your right to object to Mr. Roberts coming here; but don't call it snooping, Mr. Nichols."

Elly came racing across the yard. Darting past her father, she put a protective arm around Eudora. "Papa, don't you be cross to Miss Stoddard!" she cried.

Webb was so surprised to have one of his brood stand up to him that he stood there tongue-tied for a moment. Elly was his favorite child, and though he ruled his family with an iron hand, for her to face him unafraid filled him with a strange sense of pride.

"I didn't mean to speak rough to you, Miss Stoddard," he muttered apologetically; "but if it's just the same to you, don't ask him here again."

He stamped away, his belligerency returning with every step. Eudora had to smile to herself, for she had not expected to win a compromise from Webb so easily. She knew she had Elly to thank for it. She embraced the child affectionately.

"You're a dear, Elly!" she whispered. "I don't know how I'd make out without you."

Elly looked up at her with the sober wisdom of a woman of 40 in her eyes. "Are you going to run off and marry Clay Roberts like mama said?" she asked.

Eudora laughed to hide her confusion. "When did your mother ever say such a thing, Elly?"

"The first morning you came to breakfast. Don't you remember? She said the trouble with young schoolteachers was that they were always running off and getting married."

Eudora hugged her tighter. "Elly Nichols, what strange things go on in your little head! I'm not thinking of running off and marrying anyone. Why, I hardly know Mr. Roberts!"

Eudora's amusement faded as soon as Elly left.

What an absurd idea! she thought. *I've only seen the man twice!*

She sat down to write her aunt but her thoughts kept straying to Clay. He was so tall and straight, and his gray eyes had a way of losing all their coldness when he spoke to her. She shuddered when she remembered how close he had been to death at Skull Tanks.

"Father in Heaven, keep him safe!" she whispered. "I don't want anything to happen to him!"

When Clay left her, it was not in his mind to see Harvey before returning to the Santa Bonita. In fact, he was half a mile beyond Willow Creek before he suddenly decided to swing south and stop at the Hume ranch.

Virgil Hume was one of the very few who knew Harvey and Roberts had met secretly on several occasions. One evening, on Willow Creek, he had been present himself. He was at Harvey's place this afternoon, and when Clay rode in, he recognized him at once.

"If you're lookin' for Harvey, he'll be here in a few minutes," Virgil told him. "He's out on the flats, bringin' in a hoss. Looks like him cumin' now. Will you git down?"

"For a few minutes," Clay replied. "I suppose you heard that Nichols caught Caney's sheep on his range and turned them back."

"Yeh, heard about it this mornin'." Virgil wagged his head gravely. "There'll be some blood spilled over it. You had quite a brush with Jennings. Word came out from town a couple hours ago that Pat Redman is really bad off."

"I'm sorry to hear it," said Clay. "Getting him in to the doctor was a long, tough trip for a man in his condition. I figure if he had grit enough to stand that, he'll pull through."

Harvey joined them and shook hands with Clay. "Have you seen Miss Stoddard?" he asked.

"I just left her. I was sure you wouldn't mind riding over yesterday. I'd have come down myself and asked you, but there wasn't time; I had to pull out in a hurry." Clay grinned.

"That was some concession Big John made in coming here. But you must have got along all right; he says he's glad he saw you."

"We had quite a talk," said Harvey. "After we got started we seemed to find we had the same ideas about a good many things. I hope it's the beginning of a better understanding all the way round. If you saw Eudora this afternoon then you know how things are going with Webb and Caney. She doesn't think she's in any danger."

"I know she doesn't. She may be right; but I'm not so sure. If Caney has provocation enough, he's capable of riding over there and blasting everyone in sight."

"Mebbe so," Virgil declared skeptically. "Shad always puts up a big front that he's a wild tiger if you cross him. If you keep cases on him close enough you'll see he don't lose his head anywhere near as much as he lets on; he's always got a trick up his sleeve and figgerin' to come out a little better'n even. My place is a little far from the school for us to take Miss Stoddard in, but there's no reason why she can't stay with Harvey and his mother till this sheep trouble is settled one way or another."

"We'd be glad to have her," Harvey offered.

"That's what I told her," said Clay. "I got her to promise she would come over if there is any shooting. If there is a big blowup Harvey, I'd appreciate it if you got word to me."

"You can count on that," Harvey assured him. "That must have been quite a scrap around Skull Tanks."

"It wasn't any pushover," Clay declared dryly. "A lot of lead was thrown."

"Reckon there was," Virgil put in. "From all accounts I've heard, you had Jennings's bunch purty well trapped. How did they manage to git away?"

"The best answer I can give you, Virgil, is that we had too many generals with us. Do you know that country south of the San Carlos Swell?"

"I've never seen it," Virgil replied, "I'm shore Harvey never did either."

"Well, it's tough; and there's a lot of it," said Clay. "Steve had half a dozen men with him. I wouldn't say we had them trapped. After we lost Pat Redman, Rowan, and Cleve Johnson, we didn't have much of an edge."

He gave them a detailed account of the fight.

"I wonder what Dufors will have to say about it," Virgil remarked. "It makes him look bad, things like that goin' on and him sittin' in Mescal twiddlin' his thumbs. If I know him, he'll be hollerin' about yore takin' the law into yore own hands and how much better you'd have done if you'd called him in and let him deputize a posse."

"That'll just about be his slant now that the shooting is over," Harvey declared disparagingly. "He's always been the little fellow's great friend, to hear him tell it. He got by with that song and dance for a long time. It must gall him something terrible to find no one paying any attention to him any more."

"I'm sure it does," Clay agreed. "I don't know how he arrives at it but he holds me responsible."

"Hunh!" Virgil grunted. "You ignored him, didn't you? Wal, that's poison to a tinhorn like Dufors! He'll do you dirt if the chance ever comes his way!"

It was a prophetic warning, but Clay dismissed it carelessly. When he got back to the Santa Bonita he found Cleve sprawled out comfortably in a chair on the gallery, his right shoulder in a plaster cast.

"So, you're back?" he called to him. "Do you figure you'll live?"

"Yeh, reckon I'll make it." Cleve grinned.

"What's the latest word on Pat?"

"He'll be laid up a few weeks. You can't kill a tough old bird like him. I heard him tell Doc that it'd take more'n one slug to finish him off. He's got Deering believin' it too." Cleve gave him a puckered glance. "I saw your friend Dufors."

"My friend?" Clay queried facetiously.

"You look out for that bastard." Cleve was serious enough now. "He hates your guts, Clay. They're laughin' at him in Mescal, and that's somethin' Dufors can't stand."

"I guess I better watch my step," Clay observed lightly. "That's the second warning I've had within the hour."

"All right, have it your way!" Cleve snapped. "You may find yourself laughin' out of the other side of your mouth. Supper is on the table; you better get inside."

"What about you? Aren't you eating?"

"I've had mine. Elmer gave me somethin' to eat when I got back about an hour ago."

Clay walked into the dining-room and sat down next to Ringe. After the crew trooped out, he and Big John remained at the table. The latter got out his pipe and called for more coffee.

The twilight faded as they talked. Shorty McCarran, the kitchen swamper, stuck his head in the door and asked if he should light a lamp.

"No, we'll finish our talk in the office," Ringe told him.

He and Clay had just stepped out on the gallery, when a rider came into the yard at a driving gallop. He pulled up a few feet from the steps and looked about uncertainly as though unfamiliar with the place.

"Who is it?" Ringe called.

A light burned in the office and the stranger made for it. As the lamplight struck his face, they saw it was Harvey Hume. The manner of his coming was enough to cry trouble.

"What is it?" Clay demanded anxiously.

"Shad Caney's been shot!" Harvey caught his breath. "His wife and Jeb drove past the house with him about forty minutes ago. I sent Virgil over to Webb's place. If things don't look right there, he's going to bring Miss Stoddard back with him."

"Do you know anything about the shootin'?" Ringe questioned.

"I talked with Mrs. Caney. She says they heard the shots and she sent Jeb out to look for his father. He found him about half a mile from the house, just about where Jerusalem Creek begins swinging west. He was working along the creek this afternoon, burning off some locoweed, Mrs. Caney told me."

"When did all this happen?" Ringe asked.

"Just before sundown."

The old cowman shook his head grimly. "I can't say I'm surprised! I figured Webb would get him!"

"So did I," Harvey agreed. "But that's not what Shad says. He claims a dozen shots were fired at him by someone hiding in the creek bottom. He claims he got a fairly good look at the man and it wasn't Webb Nichols."

"I don't believe it!" Big John snorted. "Who does he say it was?"

"He isn't accusing anyone definitely; he's too smart for that. But he thinks it was you, Clay."

"The lying rat!" the old cowman burst out with an angry roar. "I see through his rotten game! He damned well knows it was Nichols, but he sees a chance to throw suspicion on you, Clay, and stir up trouble for me and the Association, figuring he can settle his score with Webb a little later!"

Clay took it easily. "It's ridiculous, saying I shot him," he declared unexcitedly. "I can account for every minute of my time this afternoon. I was talking to you and Virgil, Harvey, about sunset. I couldn't have been on Jerusalem Creek."

"Of course you couldn't. I think Mr. Ringe has called the turn. Virgil and I can give you a perfect alibi; but I suppose there'll be those who'll claim we're lined up with you and refuse to believe we're telling the truth."

"When Caney says the man who got him had to fire a dozen shots to drop him, he's giving Clay all the alibi he needs!" Ringe growled. "This man is a dead shot, Harvey; he might miss a target the first time, but not twice in a row!" He focused his irate eyes on Clay. "You got nothing to worry about. I'll cram this nonsense down Caney's gullet!"

"Where was he hit, Harvey?" Clay asked.

"In the chest. The bullet couldn't have touched a lung or he would have been bleeding more. You can depend on it that Frank Dufors will try to build this up into something. When Virgil told you Dufors would do you dirt if he got the chance, he couldn't have had this in mind, but it's the sort of thing he meant."

"You know your rights," the big man of the Santa Bonita told Clay. "Dufors doesn't want to try to question you or take you into custody unless Caney makes a charge. I don't believe Caney will go that far, he'll be satisfied to throw suspicion on you and hope that feeling against you will boil over. Harvey, will you tell me what reason Caney says Clay had for going after him?"

"I asked Mrs. Caney that very question," Harvey answered. "She said she didn't know, but young Jeb told me his father made you back down, Clay, the afternoon you rode over there with the boy's rifle and that was why you had it in for the old man."

The lie was so preposterous that Clay was hard put to express his disgust. "That's so far from the truth that a blind man could see the whole thing is a frame-up. If there was any backing down that afternoon, Caney did it. As I reported to you, John, I told him I'd accept his story that Jeb shot the cow by mistake, but if any more Diamond R cows were beefed, it wouldn't be by mistake and that we'd do something about it. I'm not going to say any more. I'll catch up a horse and go back with you, Harvey. Virgil ought to be there by the time we get down."

They flashed out of the yard. Thirty minutes later they were on the Willow Creek road. Another mile brought them to the house.

"Virgil's back," Harvey announced. "That's his horse at the rail."

Virgil was in the kitchen with Harvey's mother. He heard them ride in and stepped out to meet them.

"You can ease up," he said. "Everythin' as quiet as a graveyard over there."

He told them he had talked with Webb but hadn't found any reason for saying anything to Eudora.

"I figgered it was better not to get her worked up by tellin' her Shad had been bushwhacked."

"She must know about it," Harvey demurred.

"I don't know how," said Virgil. "The Caneys didn't pass that way goin' to town. The only way the news could have got to the ranch was for Webb to have brought it. You can be dang shore if he was mixed up in it he wouldn't be sayin' anythin' to her about it."

Clay found his point well taken. "What did Nichols have to say?"

"I didn't mention the shootin' till we'd talked for a few minutes. I figgered he might let somethin' slip, but he didn't. Even after I had spilled the beans he didn't open up much. Said that what happened to Shad Caney was no concern of his."

"Did you tell him that Caney is trying to pin the shooting on me?" Clay asked.

Virgil shook his head emphatically. "When yo're tryin' to draw a man out you don't tell him all you know. I pointed out to Webb that a lot of folks was bound to figger that he got Shad."

"What was his answer to that?"

"He said he'd be able to take care of himself."

"Virgil, you know Webb Nichols pretty well. I'm not going to ask you to commit yourself one way or the other on whether he did or didn't shoot Caney. But if you feel free to do it, I'd like to have you tell me how he acted to you."

"Wal, he's got somethin' on his mind, I'd say. He's never been so closemouthed with me before."

Harvey yanked off his saddle and flopped it on the rail with an angry thud.

"What's the use of trying to straddle the fence, Virgil? Webb went out to get Caney; you know it as well as I do!"

"If he did, I reckon he had his reasons," was

Virgil's blunt answer. "If Shad dies, it'll be murder. I don't want to see you stuck with it, Roberts, but I'm not goin' to say anythin' that can be used against Webb."

"That's all right with me," Clay said thinly. "I'm not interested in pinning it on Nichols." His face had whipped hard and flat. "Just don't try to give him a clean bill of health at my expense, Virgil!"

Chapter Twelve

Ugly Rumors

Though Eudora went over for breakfast at the usual time, she found that Webb and Verne had already eaten and left the house. Mrs. Nichols had less to say than usual. Eudora was conscious of it, and she felt that young Moroni and Elly watched her covertly.

She told herself that her friendship with Clay was at the bottom of it. The explanation satisfied her, and she thought little about it. Webb and Verne had not been at the table for supper, either. If it was their intention to show their resentment over what she had done by not sitting down to the table with her, it didn't matter to her.

It's childish, and they'll have to get over it, she thought, in dismissing it from her mind.

She had only to reach the schoolhouse, however, to be apprised at once of the attempt to slay Shad Caney. The children were babbling excitedly about it; they had heard the news at home and filled it in with details out of their own imaginations. According to their tale Caney had actually accused Clay Roberts of shooting him. They were agreed on the time and place.

Eudora was beside herself. Her faith in Clay's innocence did not waver, but she couldn't deny that he had been in the basin in the late afternoon; that after he left her he would have had ample time to reach Jerusalem Creek before sunset.

Josie Hume, Virgil's twelve-year-old daughter, seemed to have more details than the others. Eudora called her inside.

"Josie, I suppose you heard all this from your father." And when the child said yes, Eudora questioned her about how Virgil had got his information.

"He was at Uncle Harvey's place when Mrs. Caney and Jeb drove by last night, Miss Stoddard. They talked to her, and then Uncle Harvey went up to the Santa Bonita to tell Mr. Roberts. Papa says Mr. Roberts couldn't have done it, no matter what Mr. Caney says."

"Did he give any reason for saying that?" Eudora asked anxiously.

"Oh, sure! Papa says Clay Roberts was with him and Uncle Harvey when the sun went down."

"They were with him? Where, Josie?"

"At Uncle Harvey's ranch."

With a deep sigh of relief Eudora sank back in her chair, feeling so weak for a moment she didn't want to move. What did it matter what Shad Caney claimed if Clay could prove his innocence? she asked herself over and over.

Somehow, she got through the morning. The children had just been dismissed and were in the yard, when Clay rode up. He could see that Eudora was fully informed about what had happened.

"I wanted to get down here earlier, but I thought I better wait till noon," he told her. "There's no reason to worry on my account."

"How can I help it, Clay, even though I know you had nothing to do with it? Josie Hume told me you were with Harvey and her father at the time of the shooting. Will you tell me why Mr. Caney is accusing you?"

"I don't know that he is," Clay told her. "As I get it, he says he *thinks* I'm the man he saw in the brush along the creek. That's stopping some distance short of actually accusing me."

Eudora was deeply puzzled until he explained what he believed was Caney's purpose. He gazed at her soberly for a moment.

"Eudora, you must know who fired those shots. Surely, there can't be any doubt in your mind."

"I don't suppose there is," she acknowledged, after some hesitation. "But if I said anything it would be based on what I think, not on what I know."

She knew she was protecting Webb and not being completely honest with Clay. She excused it by telling herself that as long as his innocence could be easily proved he could not ask her to turn against Elly's father. Nevertheless, Webb's absence from the ranch at suppertime and the fact that when she had walked past the corral last evening the air was heavy with the pungent smell of horse sweat now had a sinister significance.

"Maybe it's just as well if you don't say anything," Clay observed thoughtfully. "Have I got your word for it, Eudora, that no one has threatened you against talking?"

"Positively! Mr. Nichols objected to your coming to the ranch. We had some words about it; but I swear to you, Clay, that I knew nothing about the shooting until I reached school this morning."

She told him what had passed between Webb and her.

"I'm glad he didn't say anything about ruling me off the road," said Clay, his tone bitingly sarcastic. "This trouble with Caney is going to make Nichols doubly determined to have me keep my distance. I don't have to hold back with you, Eudora; I believe Nichols shot Caney. He may not have been alone, either."

"Verne?" she gasped, not trying to dissemble her amazement.

"It wouldn't surprise me. Caney says he saw only one man. He may be lying about that, but his tale that a dozen shots were fired at him sounds like the truth. I don't see any reason why he should have invented it. If a dozen shots were slapped at him, someone was doing some wild shooting, and that sounds like some inexperienced kid like Verne. Tomorrow's Saturday. I don't suppose there's any chance of our spending the day up on the Ledge now."

"I don't know," she murmured uncertainly, speaking to herself as much as to him. "I suppose Uncle Dan and Aunt Jude are worried sick about me. I can write them this afternoon and send the letter over to the Humes; I guess they will find some way of sending it into town tomorrow. I'm so weary of all this fighting that I'd do most anything to get away from it for a few hours. If you'll bring a horse that won't throw me, Clay, we'll ride up in the timber tomorrow. I'll be ready whenever you say."

He was pleased, and he did not try to conceal it. "You'll see me coming about nine o'clock. I'll have the cook at the ranch fix up a picnic lunch for us. If you want to write your letter now, I'll take it over to Harvey. I thought I'd ride that way and go up through White Pine."

"That'll be better than waiting until this afternoon, if you're sure I'm not putting you out. It will take me only a few minutes to write a note."

"You needn't hurry," he told her. "I'll just wait out here at the gate."

Eudora was still inside, when Clay noticed a horseman jogging toward him from the direction of Mescal. He found nothing familiar about the rider, and it was not until the latter was within a few yards of him that he saw it was Frank Dufors.

Dufors jerked a frosty nod and pulled up his horse.

"Findin' you down here will save me some ridin'," he announced. "I want to ask you some questions, Roberts."

"Go ahead," Clay told him, his tone vaguely challenging. He was in no doubt as to what was coming. "Evidently Caney hasn't got around to openly accusing me, or you'd be flashing a warrant and putting me under arrest."

Dufors was angry instantly. "If that's your idea of beatin' me to the punch, forget it!" he snapped. "I don't propose to let the fact that Caney can't make a positive identification of the party who tried to murder him stop me from gittin' to the bottom of this business. There's always some evidence that can be dug up. When I git it, there'll be an arrest, I promise you!"

"That's very commendable, Frank—seeing you

bestirring yourself this way," Clay remarked, with maddening equanimity. "I figured you wouldn't let any grass grow under your feet when you learned there was a chance to tie this thing on me. But you go ahead."

"That's what I intend to do!" Dufors glared at him with a fierce contempt. "You been ridin' your high horse too long around here! Don't make the mistake of thinkin' that just 'cause most folks ain't got no use for Caney they're goin' to let this thing slide! I'm goin' to have a look around at the scene of the shootin', and if I find anythin', I'll know how to handle it!"

"You mean you'll know how to make the most of it," Clay countered. "I'm afraid you're playing a losing hand, Frank." His tone was deliberately patronizing. "You've waited a little too long to succeed in lifting my scalp; the old game of whipping up feeling against the Magdalena Stockmen's Association is played out. You said something about questioning me. What do you want to know?"

"You were seen down in the basin late yesterday afternoon. Do you deny it?"

"No."

"Just where were you durin' the half-hour before sunset?"

"I was at Harvey Hume's ranch—talking with him and Virgil."

"So that's the alibi you've framed up, is it?"

Dufors jeered. "Everybody knows the Humes have been lined up with you right along; nobody's goin' to believe what they have to say!"

"You better try telling that to Virgil and Harvey."

For all of his blustering and snarling Dufors was not able to conceal his chagrin at learning that Clay had an alibi.

"I'll see 'em durin' the day!" he growled. "If they're lookin' for trouble, they can be accommodated!"

Clay gave him a pitying smile. He had always considered Frank Dufors an empty-headed windbag and he had never been as sure of it as now. "You're talking big, Frank," he said thinly. "Virgil and Harvey have got your number, and you know it. You won't do much blowing off to them. But you've got some more questions for me. Go ahead with them."

Dufors's eyes narrowed murderously. He knew he was being toyed with, and it was more than he could stand. His hand dropped to his gun, threateningly. "Don't crowd me too hard!" he ground out.

Clay watched him with a deceiving carelessness; actually, Dufors had his complete attention now. "You better think it over before you draw on me," he said softly. "You know I never bluff with a gun, Frank."

Dufors was sorely tempted, but a flash of sense stayed him. The moment passed, however, and Eudora came hurrying toward them. Dufors's hand fell away from his gun and the muscles in Clay's shoulders relaxed.

Eudora was not deceived. In the yard, the children had stopped their play and were staring openmouthed at the two men. It was all the confirmation she needed.

"What is it, Clay?" she asked, her throat tight, her eyes focused sharply on the deputy sheriff.

"Nothing important," Clay replied. "Mr. Dufors was just asking me what I know about the shooting."

Dufors was willing enough to let it go at that.

"Your uncle asked me to bring a letter out to you, Miss Stoddard," he informed Eudora. "The old couple are a little worried about you."

He produced the letter and handed it to her.

"It was kind of you to bother," she said.

Dufors nodded. "Glad to be able to do you a favor. I told Dan he and the missus had no reason to be alarmed. I'll see him when I git back and tell him I found you all right."

He raised a hand to his hat and rode on without a word to Roberts.

Eudora turned anxiously to the letter as soon as they were alone. "Clay—that man was at the point of drawing his gun on you!"

"No, he just thought he was, Eudora. It's

never been Dufors's policy to toe the line with anyone when the chances were even. That's why he had to leave Texas. He knows that I know it, and if you went deep enough, I guess you'd find that's the real reason for his bile against me. The roof fell in on him when I told him I was with Virgil and Harvey last evening."

"Clay, that man is dangerous, I don't care what you say!" Eudora insisted. "Please don't take him so lightly. It was just your great good fortune that you happened to turn back last evening to see Harvey."

To see her so concerned on his account, so near and so lovely, set his pulse to pounding. The hardness left his mouth and he smiled at her fondly.

"Don't be afraid for me; I'll be careful," he said, a strange huskiness in his voice. "Dufors is going over to Jerusalem Creek. He won't find anything to fasten on me. He'll talk loud for a few days, and that'll be the end of it. Do you want to read the letter he brought before I go? You may want to add something to yours."

Eudora glanced over her aunt's letter and then read it aloud.

"Aunt Jude worries so!" she exclaimed. "I couldn't give up the school now. I honestly don't believe I'm in any danger. And I do owe it to the children to finish out the term. It's such a short time now."

"I've been thinking of that," he confessed, his gray eyes suddenly sober. "It's going to be a short time for both of us; a few weeks more and my job will be finished. As for your giving up the school, it's foolish even to suggest it; if I know you at all, you'll stick it out no matter what happens. I'm sure that whenever you feel it's your duty to do something, that ends it."

"I'm not just being stubborn, Clay—"

"Of course not! You've got courage. It's one of the things about you I admire most. I don't see how there can be any more trouble between Caney and Nichols until Caney gets back on his feet. That may take some time."

"Is Mr. Caney out of danger?" Eudora asked.

"Dufors didn't say. He would have been sure to mention it if the news was bad."

Eudora started to speak but checked herself.

"What is it?" Clay queried.

"I know you won't approve," she answered, "but I'm going to walk over to the Caneys this afternoon; Cissy and Lorenzo are there alone. They're just children, Clay."

"If you think you can ease their minds it's all right with me. It's kind and thoughtful of you, though I don't believe Nichols will appreciate it."

"I imagine Mr. Nichols won't have too much to say to me," Eudora remarked confidently.

Clay let it pass without comment, but as he rode away, he found it sticking in his mind.

"She's got something on Nichols," he told himself. "That's why she isn't afraid to face up to him."

He was convinced that it had to do with the bushwhacking on Jerusalem Creek. A smile brushed his mouth as he thought of Webb trying to match wits with her.

"Nichols will either toe the line or find himself in hot water," he mused. "And there won't be any mystery left about who shot Shad Caney!"

Chapter Thirteen

Captured!

In Mescal, whether on foot or mounted, overalls and a mannish-looking shirt were popular attire for young women of Eudora's age. It followed that she soon was wearing Western garb. Topped off with a wide-brimmed Stetson, with a buckskin throatlatch dangling beneath her chin, she found it a becoming outfit. Until today, however, she had never appreciated how practical it was.

Clay gazed at her admiringly, as they made the long climb up Cochinilla Wash.

"I must say you don't look anything like a prim little schoolmarm in that rig," he said happily. "Nor an Eastern tenderfoot, either. The way you sit that saddle it won't be no trick to make a rider out of you. This is a long uphill trail, but we've got most of it behind us. You're not getting tired?"

"Not a bit! I'm enjoying every moment. I feel as though I could go on forever."

"I'm afraid that would be overdoing it a little," Clay said laughingly. "We've the day ahead of us. When we reach the timber, we'll

174

locate a spring and have lunch; we can do some exploring this afternoon. There's one place I want to show you after the sun gets around to the west; you'll be able to see all the way to the Colorado."

It was a day that Eudora was long to remember. The pine-scented air was like wine. Even more precious was the peace and quiet of the high forest and the companionship of the tall man at her side. Magdalena Basin, with its strife and grim faces, seemed far away.

It was high noon before Clay found a flowing spring. He made a tiny squaw fire and boiled coffee and barbecued thin strips of fresh beef. Eudora watched him with interest.

"You do everything so easily," she said. "And quickly too. I suppose you've lived outdoors most of your life."

"Ever since I was a boy. I've been on the move most of the time. I haven't missed much between Texas and the Coast."

"Having seen it all, what part of it suits you best, Clay?"

"That would depend on what I wanted from it. I've thought some of starting a spread of my own some day. I'm a Texan and if I was to go in for cattle, Texas would be the place for me. In a weak moment some years ago I bought a mine out in northern Nevada. It's country that appeals to me."

175

"And the mine?"

"I've worked it some—two or three months at a time. I built a comfortable cabin on the claim. At least, it was comfortable the last time I was there. I've never taken a dollar out of the mine but I haven't gone far enough— I guess we can eat; everything seems to be ready."

The long ride had given Eudora an appetite. She found the simple fare delicious, and praised the cook. For the first time in weeks she was lighthearted and carefree.

Clay responded to her mood and his laughter had a warm ring. He had said nothing about his surmise that Eudora knew more about Webb's connection with the Caney affair than she had told him, and he had no intention of bringing it up. That morning, however, Eudora had not been waiting at the gate, as he had rather expected. Deliberately, he felt, she had remained in her cabin, so that he might ride up to her door. Clay considered it a complete confirmation of his contention.

After they had finished lunch, Clay washed his pans and put out the fire before he sat down beside her and rolled a cigarette.

"Before we leave here we'll walk out on the rock cap and have a look at the Desolations," he said. "If you like mountains, there's a lot of them, and they climb up into the air pretty high." He glanced at his watch. "Not quite two yet."

"Clay, that's a beautiful fob you wear on your watch. Might I see it?"

"Certainly. I've had it a long time."

"Indian, isn't it?" Eudora queried, as she laid it flat in her palm.

"A Navaho silversmith in Santa Fe made it for me. If you like it, I'll trade you for it," he offered banteringly. "That bracelet, with all those Columbian half dollars jingling, would suit me fine."

"It wouldn't be a fair trade," Eudora insisted. "They were making bracelets at the fair, in Chicago, so I had to have one. It really isn't worth anything, Clay."

"It would be worth a lot to me," he said, suddenly sober.

"All right, it's a trade then! You'll have to have the bracelet made over before you can use it as a fob."

"That won't be much of a trick. I can do it myself. I'll be wearing it the next time you see me."

Their hands touched as they made the exchange. That accidental contact left them tense and silent for several minutes.

"Have you made any plans about where you're going when you leave the basin?" she asked.

"Only one, Eudora. When I leave here, I don't want to go alone. I told you the other day I could hang up my guns and turn to something else. I meant I could do it for you. I'm sure about this, Eudora! I know how much I'm asking; you're so lovely, and I have so little to offer. But for whatever it's worth, my life is yours!"

Breathless, she gazed at him with surrender in her eyes. "Darling, don't put it that way!" she whispered. "You're all I want! Everything! You know I love you, Clay!"

With his strong arms straining her close, she raised her mouth to his. The world stood still for both of them and the moments fled unnoticed.

Eudora looked up at him and laid her hand tenderly against his cheek. "You'll stay on at the Santa Bonita until school is over?"

"Of course! We can be married in Mescal. I'd like to take you back to Texas for a few weeks. I haven't any close relatives back there but I've got a lot of old friends. Afterward, if it's agreeable to you, we can go out to Nevada for the rest of the summer. If the mine doesn't begin to show something by the time snow flies, I'll sell it."

Eudora found his plans alluring and exciting. That they were to be together was all that really mattered to her. The long afternoon passed as in a dream.

Twilight was upon them as they retraced their way down the wash.

"I'm afraid we've done ourselves out of

supper," Clay declared. "We could cross the basin by way of White Pine and get something to nibble on at the store. I've got pretty well acquainted with Eph Adkins; he might go so far as to offer us a cup of coffee."

Eudora fell in with the suggestion, and they turned toward White Pine. The stars were out by the time they reached the store. Old Eph welcomed them, however, and insisted on taking them into his kitchen and cooking bacon and eggs.

This was Eph's first meeting with Eudora. He found her as attractive as rumor had painted her. Behind his shrewd eyes, his mind was busy, and after he had said good night to them, he stood on the store steps ruminating. "They ain't sayin' nuthin'," he cackled to himself, "but they has shore taken an awful shine to each other!"

"We fared better than I expected," Clay remarked, as he rode along at Eudora's side. "Eph isn't a bad sort."

Eudora surprised him with a question.

"Do you trust him, Clay?"

"No, not particularly," was his laughing response. "Whatever made you bring that up?"

"I don't know," she answered, shaking her head as though to throw off some unpleasant thought. "His eyes are shifty and full of little schemes. I don't like people whose eyes are never still. They're usually slippery customers."

Her use of the homely expression, as much as her opinion of Eph, brought a broad grin to Clay's face. "I don't imagine Eph gives anyone sixteen ounces to the pound."

It was late, when they passed the schoolhouse.

"Almost home," Clay said. "Suppose we walk the rest of it; you're too far away, in that saddle."

He helped her down and took her in his arms. Her eyes were wet against his cheek.

"Why the tears, Eudora?" he murmured.

"No reason. Just too happy, I guess. When will I be seeing you again, Clay?"

"In a day or two, or sooner, unless something comes up, and I don't believe anything will; the rustling is over."

The days that followed seemed to bear him out; news filtered into the big ranch on the Santa Bonita daily but no one reported having seen any sign of the Jennings gang. Pat Redman had been brought home and was on the mend. Clay met Eudora several times during the week and learned from her that Shad Caney was back at his ranch. Dufors's attempt to exploit the shooting had not met with any success.

"He couldn't get anybody to go along with him after it got around that you were with Virgil and me," Harvey Hume told Clay, when they met by chance as the former was returning from White Pine, late one afternoon. "I haven't heard a peep out of him since he dropped by last Friday afternoon. I gather that Dufors would like to forget the whole business. He may be thick, but he must have sense enough to realize there'll be some further developments that'll make him look foolish over what he tried to do. Oh, you don't have to look so blank about it, Clay! Shad knows who cut him down; as soon as he feels strong and sassy, he'll do something about it."

"In the meantime, what do you think Nichols is going to be doing?" Clay inquired pointedly. "He knows Caney has a real score to settle with him now. But if they blow each other's head off it'll be all right with me if they'll just wait until the school term is over and Eudora is back in Mescal. I'll be through in a couple of weeks myself."

"I suppose you will," Harvey acknowledged regretfully. "You don't hear anything more of Jennings?"

"Not a word. I imagine Steve knows where to find the pickings better than they are here."

When they parted, Clay continued across the basin, stopping at White Pine for a few minutes on the chance that Eph's gossip might hold something of interest. It was time wasted, and the sun was down before he forded the Santa Bonita, several miles below the house.

The brush grew high close to the crossing, but he was so near home and so familiar with the spot that he was not suspicious of it. His horse started to splash across the creek at a walk, head lowered as it tried to nuzzle the water.

"Go on, drink if you want to!" Clay muttered, letting the animal have its head.

The moment was made to order for the man who had been waiting to intercept him at the crossing. In his most optimistic calculations he had not hoped to catch Clay so completely off guard.

"Freeze right there, Roberts!" he commanded. "I got you covered!"

The only weapon Clay was wearing was the forty-five on his hip. He turned his head an inch or two and scanned the brush on his right and found a rifle trained on him.

"Looks like you're calling the tune," he said tightly, knowing it was too late to reach for his gun.

"Yeh!" the other grunted. "Unbuckle yore gun belt and let it drop!"

Clay could do nothing but oblige.

The man in the brush was mounted. He pushed out into the open. He said, "I reckon you don't know me, Roberts. I'm Slick Carroll. This ain't no ordinary stick-up; you won't have no trouble with me if you do what I tell you. Back off a few feet and I'll pick up yore gun."

They watched each other intently as the operation was performed. Carroll hung the wet gun belt on his saddle horn. He was tall and wiry, with a hard-bitten face, his eyes cold and emotionless. Clay could understand why Steve Jennings found the man invaluable.

"Turn up the crick," the rustler ordered. "I'll drill you if you try to bust away from me."

He called a halt as soon as they were a safe distance east of the ford.

"No use wastin' words," he jerked out. "Steve's in tough shape; he needs a doctor damned bad!"

Some of the tightness left Clay's mouth. "What's the proposition?" he inquired.

"I'll let Steve put it to you; it ain't too long a ride. We sent up to Brown's Park for Sawbones Parker. We got word today that he's in the jug in Laramie City. Let's git movin'!"

Chapter Fourteen

Impromptu Surgery

Clay had often heard of George Parker, the renegade doctor, who had been patching up outlaws for a dozen years. Brown's Park, tucked away on the Green River, in the northwest corner of Colorado, where Utah, Wyoming, and Colorado come together, was a popular owlhoot rendezvous, and the men who wintered there, or sought its sanctuary, when the law was hot on their heels, had carried tales about Sawbones Parker's skill across half a dozen states.

"I don't know of any deal I can make with Steve," Clay remarked as they rode along. "I don't suppose it would do me any good to refuse to go."

Carroll shrugged. "Why mention it, Roberts? I didn't take this chance for nothin'."

Their way led up Cochinilla Wash and across the Ledge. Clay could see the Desolations rearing up ahead of them.

"Are we going over the pass?" he asked.

"I know where we're goin'," was the

184

unenlightening answer. "Just hold yore shirt on."

In the course of an hour, Carroll swung off sharply to the north. They hadn't proceeded very far before he reined in and raised his voice in an excellent imitation of the gray owl's long-drawn cry. It was answered promptly.

"All right, Roberts; we go up over this rock slide," Carroll announced.

Another 500 yards brought them to the narrow mouth of a small box canyon. Clay found the canyon widening almost as soon as they were past the portal. The man who had answered Carroll's signal joined them and they broke through high brush and passed under tall pines. Presently, there was grass underfoot.

That means water, Clay thought. *Water, firewood and grass enough to keep your horses strong—a man couldn't ask for more in the way of a hideout.* He knew he had been within a quarter of a mile of this hidden canyon without ever suspecting it was here.

A low fire glowed in the distance. Someone threw dry brush on it as they advanced and the fire blazed up. Jennings lay on his blanket; his men lounged near, hands close to their guns.

Carroll slid to the ground and motioned for Clay to get down. He turned to Steve then. "Here's Roberts," he said. "I told him you had a proposition to make; I didn't say what."

"Bring him over," Jennings ordered, his voice rough with pain. His face was deeply lined and haggard in the firelight.

"You're in tough shape, Steve," Clay said, squatting down on his heels beside him. "Does this go back to the trouble we had at Skull Tanks?"

"Yeh! I been goin' through hell for a few days. I'm a goner if I don't get a doctor in a hurry. It's my right leg; puffin' up to beat hell. Blood poison, I reckon."

"You shouldn't have waited so long," Clay told him. "Carroll told me you sent for Sawbones Parker."

"I kept on figurin' he'd come. It's just my luck the damned fool would have to get snagged in a train holdup. But that's cold turkey now! I know I can get a square deal from you, Clay; get the doctor out here from Mescal in a hurry and have him fix me up, and I'll give you my word we won't never molest another stockman in Arizona."

Clay realized that Slick and the others were hanging on his answer. Slowly, he shook his head. "I couldn't get away with it, Steve," he said soberly.

"Why not?"

"Ringe, Pat Redman—not a one of them would stand for it. Your word would be good enough for me, but not for them; I never could make them see it, Steve. I can see how you're suffering. Have you been filling up with whisky to get away from it?"

"No, not a drop."

"You stay away from it." Clay reached out and put his hand on Steve's damp forehead. "You've got a high fever. If you've got any sense in you, let me take you in—"

"And be sent up for the rest of my life?"

"The rest of your life may be a matter of just a couple of days if something isn't done for you." Clay turned to Carroll. "Have you cut the slug out?"

"Not a chance! He wouldn't let us touch him!"

Clay straightened up, his face as grave as those ringed around him. "What's the use of telling you he's going to be all right? You know I'd be lying; you can see the shape he's in; he's let this thing go till his life is hanging in the balance. If you boys have any drag with him, I advise you to make him change his mind about letting me take him in. We can tie him in his saddle. I'll put him in a wagon at the Santa Bonita and have him in Mescal by daylight. I promise you he'll be fairly treated."

"He won't listen to me!" Slick growled. "Mebbe you can talk him into it, Utah!"

Utah Sims, a pint-size little man, shook his head. "Nobody makes up Steve's mind for

187

him. If you want to do somethin' for him, Roberts, why can't you git the doctor out here on yore own hook and tell Big John and the rest of 'em about it afterward?"

"Do you think I could get Doctor Deering to come on those terms?" Clay countered. "You ought to know he wouldn't; he's got to go on making a living out of his doctoring in these parts. Don't expect him to do anything that would put him in wrong with the members of the Association."

"You're right, Clay," Steve muttered. "If I got to die, I'll do my dyin' here," he added grimly. "I'd just as soon be dead as spend twenty to thirty years in that rattrap in Florence."

Carroll motioned for Clay to walk over to the fire with him. "There's some meat in the pot; might as well have a bite to eat." He glanced back at Steve and shook his head. "I'd feel as he does about givin' myself up. We can't move him; it means we'll have to keep you here."

Clay nodded woodenly. He declined anything to eat. With a preoccupied air, he sipped a cup of hot coffee.

"Who does the cooking in your outfit?" he asked.

"We all take a hand at it," said Carroll.

"Build up the fire, then, and put some water on to boil. I'll need a couple pots of it. Have you got a sharp barlow knife among you?"

"Yeh, I've got one." Slick eyed him darkly. "What's the idea?"

"I'm going to make Steve a proposition of my own. You better put a running iron in the fire to heat. Come on! We'll see what he's got to say about it!"

He walked briskly back to where Jennings lay. "Steve, let me have a look at that leg. Something's got to be done for you." Without waiting for the outlaw's consent, he told Carroll and the others to pick Jennings up in his blanket and carry him over to the fire.

"Somebody better put a slug into me and have it over with," Steve groaned. "I can't stand any more of this!"

"You'll stand it!" Clay rapped. "You used to have some guts, Steve. It isn't going to hurt you any to let me look at your leg."

With Carroll's knife, he cut away the blood-stained bandage. A sickening smell rose from the badly infected wound.

"Looks bad, eh?" Jennings questioned weakly.

"It's rotten. Steve, you listen to me. You offered me a deal, now I'm going to offer you one. I'm not a doctor, but I've picked up enough buckshot surgery in my time to know what to do for your leg. There's poison working through your system. It may be too late for the best man in the world to help you. All I'm offering you is a chance, and it's the only one you've

189

got. I'll do the best I can if you'll agree to the rest of the bargain."

"Well?"

"I want your word that I'll be free to leave tomorrow, and I'm to go with the distinct understanding that I'll be back forty-eight hours later with a posse to round you up if you haven't cleared out. That'll give you two days in which to gather strength enough to move on."

Every man in the rustler camp had heard the proposition. They held their eyes on Jennings, waiting for his answer.

"I'll pass you my word on that," Steve muttered. "I know you'll shoot square with me."

Clay's preparations were simple. He sterilized the knife in boiling water and washed his hands carefully. The men found several clean undershirts in their saddlebags. He tore them into strips.

"It's going to take three or four of you to hold him down," he told them. "Don't let him get away from you."

Knowing how sore the wound was, Clay tried his best to be careful as he started to wash it out. At the first touch of hot water, Jennings stiffened convulsively. The groan of pain died on his lips suddenly and he fell back limply.

"He's out cold!" Carroll growled.

"Good," Clay responded. "He won't feel the rest of this."

He worked quickly now, removing the disintegrated tissue before he started probing for the bullet. The point of the knife blade touched the leaden pellet. He lost it three or four times before he was able to extract it.

The wound was bleeding freely. Jennings was still unconscious.

"Get that iron out of the fire and let me have it in a hurry!" Clay rapped.

The point of the running iron was white hot when Utah Sims handed it to him. Clay knocked off the ashes that clung to it and slapped it down on Steve's leg. There was an immediate smell of scorched flesh. Carroll turned away, sick to his stomach.

With the wound cauterized, nothing remained to be done but bind it up.

"We'll carry him away from the fire now," said Clay. "For the rest of the night I want cold compresses put on his head. It's the best we can do to check his fever."

The spring water was ice-cold. Clay washed Steve's face. The latter opened his eyes but slipped back into unconsciousness almost at once.

"We'll have to take turns at this," Clay told the men. "Just dip the cloth into the water, wring it out, and fold it over his forehead. Come on, Utah; you can be the first."

Clay sat down on a log and lighted a cigarette.

"What do you think, Roberts?" Slick asked, his face still a bilious yellow.

"We won't be able to tell for a few hours. If his heart is strong enough, he ought to make it."

Jennings had several lucid intervals during the night. Clay was with him at daylight. His patient was perspiring freely, which he took for a good sign, and the wound was draining.

Steve watched him with puckered eyes. "Beats hell—you bein' here and takin' care of me."

"Yeh," Clay agreed. "I wouldn't expect any stockman to understand it. I know what it'll do to my professional reputation if it gets noised around; I'll be accused of being in cahoots with you on the quiet. You're still running a high fever, but you seem to be holding your own. I'll stick around until evening."

By noon, Steve had improved enough to take a little nourishment. When he asked for a cigarette, Clay lighted one for him. The outlaw smiled his thanks.

"We've come a long way since we first met," he said. "I know this was for old times' sake, Clay. I won't forget it."

"I wish you would, Steve; you know what I

192

told you this morning. You get a little sleep when you finish that smoke."

Jennings slept most of the afternoon. It was after five when Clay told him he was pulling out.

"It'll take me three hours to get down to the ranch. You'll be all right if you go easy; don't let them move you tomorrow."

Carroll rode down to the mouth of the canyon with him. "Reckon you can find yore way back," he said.

"Yeh! You've got forty-eight hours."

"Okay," Slick muttered. "That ought to be time enough."

When he rode into the yard at the Santa Bonita, Big John came out to meet him. He was not his usual phlegmatic self.

"Where have you been, Clay?" the big man asked at once.

"Across the ledge and beyond. I've located Jennings's bunch. They're holed up in box canyon; Steve is in tough shape. There's no hurry about going after them; we can organize a strong posse tomorrow and go up the following day."

"That's good news!" Ringe declared. "We'll play our cards close to our vest this time and see if we can't round 'em up. You haven't had supper?"

"No—"

"Neither have I; I just got back from town. The basin is in an uproar again. Shad Caney's son Jeb was killed sometime during the afternoon."

"What!" Clay's head went up and his mouth turned hard. "Don't tell me they're going to try to pin this job on me too! I didn't have anything against the kid!"

"If you did, you wouldn't lay out to kill him," Big John jerked out fiercely. "No one's being accused yet. The boy was tending the old man's sheep when it happened. You know where that little knoll rises on the north side of the road, about two miles east of the schoolhouse?" Clay nodded. "Someone hid out on the knoll and got the lad from there. Some folks say he was killed by mistake; that it was his old man who was to have been rubbed out. Jeb was wearing one of Shad's hats; he and the boy were about the same size."

Clay's thoughts winged to Eudora. "I'll have to grab a bite to eat in a hurry, John; I've got to go down to the basin this evening!"

Ringe understood why Clay found his going so imperative. "That young woman's got a lot of grit and common sense, Clay; if I've got things sized up correctly, you'll find her more concerned about you than herself."

"I don't doubt it," Clay acknowledged gravely. "It doesn't ease my nerves any. The last time I saw Harvey, we talked about Caney and Nichols. He was of the opinion that Caney wouldn't waste any time about getting even for that business on Jerusalem Creek. I reminded Harvey that Nichols wouldn't let the grass grow under his feet, either, knowing Shad was certain to try to square his account. This seems to bear it out."

"Then you figure it was Webb, and he killed the boy by mistake—"

"I do not! Jeb wasn't killed by mistake. Just as sure as we're standing here, Webb Nichols sent Verne out to git that kid!"

"Huh!" Big John grunted grimly. "I wonder if that's the way it was!"

Chapter Fifteen

A Murder Confession

Four days later, Roberts, Big John, and Coconino Williams followed a wagon into town, with a Diamond R puncher handling the team. Steve Jennings lay weak and helpless in the wagon.

Doc Deering examined him before he was lodged in jail and pronounced him suffering from almost complete physical collapse.

When Clay had led the posse to the box canyon, he had found it deserted, as he expected. Picking up the gang's trail had not been too difficult. Its general direction left no doubt that the rustlers were retreating into Utah.

Just before night fell, the posse had found Steve. He was alone; realizing he was too weak to continue, he had ordered Carroll and the others to save their own hides and leave him behind. He had Clay to thank that he was in Mescal, alive, for Ed Stack had wanted him strung up on the nearest tree.

With a prisoner of Steve Jennings's caliber, in his custody, Frank Dufors suddenly became an important figure again. Temporarily, the clamor over the killing of Jeb was over-shadowed. But Dufors had no intention of permitting it to die down. Mart Singer, the town constable, was impressed to guard the prisoner, so that Dufors might be free to give his time and attention to the murder. He visited the Caney ranch several times and spent hours at the scene of the killing, failing, however, to uncover anything remotely resembling a clue. His failure to find any evidence didn't discourage him, for he was not intent on solving the crime; he had his man picked out, and he didn't propose to let him slip through his fingers this time.

Though he publicly scoffed at the whisper that Clay Roberts, stung by Shad's blundering attempt to fasten the Jerusalem Creek shooting on him, had killed Jeb in revenge, he not only managed to spread it but found ways to enlarge on it.

Clay expected Caney to take it up. To his surprise Shad remained grimly silent. Harvey Hume had an explanation.

"He's keeping quiet because he knows who got Jeb; he doesn't like you any better than he did, but he isn't interested in seeing you accused; he wants the killing charged up where it belongs, Clay. I went up to the funeral after you left here yesterday. I talked with Shad before I came home. I can tell you he's a changed man; the fire's all gone out of him and he just sits around, brooding."

"Was Eudora at the services?" Clay asked.

"Yes, she was there. Has she heard anything about this talk against you?"

"She hasn't mentioned it." Clay's eyes were unconsciously bleak. "She will hear it, of course. She's deeper than you might think. It's barely two weeks to the end of school; she could come over with you and your mother for that time easily enough. But she won't consider it; she says she's got to remain where she is."

"Did she give you a reason?"

Clay shook his head. "I can only guess at it."

"She's awfully fond of little Elly. That may have something to do with it."

"She's got a better reason than that, Harvey. I'm on my way over to see her now. I better be moving; school will be out before I get there."

Eudora waved to him from the schoolhouse door as he was tethering his horse at the fence. The children had left for the day. With a glad cry she surrendered herself to his embrace.

"Hold me tight, Clay!" she whispered. "You're never out of my thoughts, my darling! Will I spoil you, telling you such things?"

"Terribly! I'm just running over with conceit already." In quite another tone, he said, "I wish we were leaving for Texas this evening.

I've got the longest two weeks of my life ahead of me—waiting!"

They sat down and talked across Eudora's desk.

"The Association paid me up in full this morning," he said. "Ringe grinned when I told him I'd like to stay on at the ranch for another two weeks."

"Did you tell him why you were staying, Clay?"

"I didn't have to! He guessed the reason. He said he'd been figuring for some time that the board would have to look for a new teacher for the fall term. John Ringe is a good man, Eudora. I wouldn't want a better friend; he's like a rock—solid and reliable."

Eudora had always admired Big John, but she had a more important matter on her mind this afternoon. She looked up, a great soberness in her blue eyes.

"Clay—Elsie Tulliver told me this noon that her father says there's talk going around that you shot Jeb. Have you heard it?"

"I have," he acknowledged. "I was hoping it wouldn't get to you. There's nothing to it."

"I know there isn't! My heavens, Clay, you don't think I doubt it, do you? I know you, darling! You would never resort to anything like that no matter what the provocation!"

"Is that the only reason—your faith in me?"

The question took Eudora by surprise. "Why—isn't that enough?" she asked, trying to hide her confusion.

"It's enough for me," Clay replied. "It might not be enough for a jury."

Her face paled and she gazed at him with a sudden tightening of her throat. "You can't mean that seriously, Clay; that you might have to face a jury, I mean?"

"No, I don't believe it will get to that. But something's going to be done about murdering that boy. The county is offering a thousand-dollar reward for information leading to the arrest and conviction of the killer. I heard this afternoon that some newspaper in Tucson is offering five hundred more. I ran into the Jennings gang. I was riding up in the hills that afternoon. Unfortunately I can't prove it. If I could get them to testify to it, they'd be discredited witnesses before they opened their mouths; no one would believe them."

There were other reasons why he couldn't avail himself of that alibi. What had transpired in the box canyon with Steve and his men could be twisted into damaging evidence if it came out now.

"I think we're worrying needlessly," Eudora said bravely.

It sounded convincing enough, but she was immediately sorry she had said it. She knew

Clay was regarding her closely. In a vague feeling of panic, she got up and walked over to the window, where she stood with her back to him. He followed and turned her around and tilted her chin.

"Eudora, let's stop this fencing." His tone was sterner than he had ever used with her. "When Shad Caney was shot, you got hold of something that Webb Nichols was afraid to face. I think that's what is happening this time. You're not saying all you know, Eudora. If you've got a reason for not being frank with me, it must be a powerful one."

"Clay—you'll have to let me be the judge of that!" she got out desperately. "You know my first loyalty is to you!"

"I couldn't go on if I thought otherwise," he said tensely. "I'm not going to try to drag the truth out of you."

He let her go and reached for his hat. Eudora ran to him and caught his hands.

"Clay, don't go like this! You're angry with me, darling! That man Dufors is behind this vicious gossip; he's so discredited we don't have to fear him!"

His sternness faded as her arms went around his neck. "Maybe we don't," he said, "but there's fifteen hundred dollars riding on this case now, and I don't know of anything Frank Dufors wouldn't do for fifteen hundred dollars."

Eudora winced. "It's cruel of you to frighten me by saying such things. I know you don't mean to."

Clay didn't attempt to press her further. He could have told her that if she had any evidence implicating either Webb or his son, or both, in the killing of young Caney, and they knew it, that she was playing a dangerous game in holding the sword of her silence over their heads, whatever her reason.

Had he been aware of the truc situation, and how deeply she was committed to it, he would have insisted on her leaving the Nichols ranch at once. It wasn't only a bit of evidence Eudora had, but Verne's detailed confession that he had killed Jeb. On the day following the shooting, shortly after supper, Verne had come to her cabin with some vague excuse for his presence, his real purpose being to discover if she suspected him and, if so, for what reason.

Eudora had bluntly accused him of the crime and in a few minutes forced some damaging admissions from Verne. Stricken with fear, when he realized how he had given himself away, he tried to recant, but his floundering only entangled him deeper than ever. In snivelling panic, he had finally blurted out the whole miserable story.

He had been riding the line and had seen

Jeb with the sheep. He had made his way back to the road and had reached the knoll by passing the schoolhouse. His father had known nothing about it, he swore.

Eudora could believe that part of it, but it did not excuse Webb Nichols in her eyes; the slaying was only an expression of the hatred with which he had been filling Verne's mind since early childhood. For the boy himself, she had a deep pity. It was strong enough to make her promise him she would keep his secret unless the law charged some innocent man with the crime.

Walking back to the ranch this afternoon Clay and Eudora were so careful to avoid saying anything about what was uppermost in their minds that each was aware of the other's restraint.

From a clump of buckbrush Verne spied on them as they passed. He had been watching them for several days, hounded by an ever mounting fear that Eudora would give him away.

He was at her door soon after Clay left. His eyes had a harried look and his mouth twitched nervously.

"You been telling him anything about me?" he demanded, when she permitted him to enter.

Eudora faced him with quick indignation. "Don't you dare to take that truculent tone with me, Verne! I gave you my promise that not a word would pass my lips unless—"

"I don't care what you tell Roberts!" he interrupted angrily. "Tell him anything you please! I was just making up what I said to you about Jeb! Scaring you, that's what I was doing!"

Under Eudora's coldly accusing glance, he dropped his eyes and began to scrape his boots.

"Is this what your father has advised you to tell me?" she demanded sternly.

"No!" Verne got out chokingly. "He don't know I blabbed anything to you! If you try to say anything ag'in me, folks will know you're doing it to keep Roberts out of trouble 'cause you're stuck on him!"

This, certainly, was the reasoning of Webb Nichols; Verne was not equal to anything as artful. Eudora regarded the boy with a disconcerting smile.

"If that's the case, Verne, then it doesn't matter whether I repeat what you told me. Since you were only having some sport at my expense, I shall feel free to say whatever I please."

It knocked all the arrogance and bluff out of Verne. Never too sharp-witted, he was helpless as consternation overcame him.

"You promised you wouldn't say nothing," he whined, a wild light in his eyes.

"Then you weren't lying to me," Eudora challenged.

"I—I don't know what I said," he faltered. "You got it out of me; I didn't mean to tell you."

Eudora was torn between pity and contempt for him. It was well enough to hold his father responsible for what Verne had done, but the boy was weak and treacherous on his own account.

"You get out of here, Verne," she ordered, "and don't come again. You can tell your father I'll do my best not to betray you. If he has anything further to say about it, he'll have to speak to me himself."

She locked the door after Verne left and tried to reduce her racing thoughts to ordered thinking. It was true, she realized, if a trumped-up charge was brought against Clay and she rushed to aid him with her story that every word she had to say would be put down as prejudiced in his favor. It would be brought out that she and Clay planned to marry. Her love for him would be used to discredit her testimony. She knew from what had just happened that Verne would repudiate his confession. And he'd be carefully coached before he was put on the stand. It would be her word against his, with Clay's fate hanging in the balance.

"I'll make the jury believe me!" was her anguished thought. "I'll find a way to bring out the truth!"

With a blessed sigh of relief she suddenly realized that there wasn't any charge against Clay as yet; no single bit of evidence.

"I'm foolish to go to pieces like this!" she told herself. "Mr. Nichols must think it's Verne who is in danger, or he wouldn't have sent him to me with such a ridiculous story!"

Had something been turned up that pointed to Verne? Or did Nichols have reason to believe such a disclosure was about to be made? She felt sure that Frank Dufors would conceal any evidence he discovered unless it could be used against Clay. But there was Shad Caney; he might have found something, and he was no longer playing Dufors's game.

Eudora sat there pondering over it for minutes on end. Clay had urged her repeatedly to leave the Nichols place and go over to the Humes'. She had refused to consider it, feeling she was perfectly safe where she was. Somehow, that sense of security had fled. It wasn't only Verve's spying and insolence; Webb's manner had been growing increasingly threatening. Mrs. Nichols and the children, with the exception of Elly, were no longer friendly. Something sinister seemed to hang over the ranch. Sitting down to the table with them and pretending there was nothing wrong had become more than she could bear.

"Clay was right; I should have gone to Harvey's several weeks ago!"

The admission, once made, cleared away any lingering doubts about what she should do. She glanced around the comfortable, homelike cabin. It was meaningless now.

I'll leave some things for Elly, she thought. *It won't take me long to pack what I want! I'll go to the Humes' this evening; Harvey can come for my trunk tomorrow!*

Chapter Sixteen

A Rotten Deal

In the bright, noontime sunshine Frank Dufors jogged up to the store at White Pine and munched on crackers and cheese and a can of mustard sardines, using Eph's counter for a table.

Old Eph had known Dufors for years and had always been cunning enough to give him the idea that they saw eye to eye. All the gossip and surmises regarding the killing of young Jeb had reached Eph in due course. He had some conclusions of his own, which he had kept to himself. This opportunity to hear what the deputy sheriff had to say about the murder found him lending an attentive ear. To his disappointment, however, Dufors had more to say about the effort he was making to solve the mystery than about what he had accomplished. His failure to make any progress had begun to nettle him and loosen his tongue.

"It's a hard nut to crack, Eph!" he declared, spearing a sardine with the blade of his pocket-knife. "You hear all the talk. How does it look to you?"

Adkins shrugged. "I dunno," he said cagily. "It might not be healthy to say too much."

Dufors shot a shrewd glance at him. "Meanin' that gent up at the Santa Bonita?"

"Meanin' it might not be healthy for me to say yes or no to anythin'," Eph returned coolly. "He don't seem able to account for where he was that afternoon. Says he was up in the hills. It kinda leaves him wide open—if you want to take it that way. I ain't sayin' I do. Why he'd want to knock off that kid, unless it was done by mistake, gits me. It was a bright, sunshiny afternoon. Don't seem as how a man wouldn't know who he was shootin' at."

"Don't let nobody tell you a mistake was made," Dufors said, with a knowing leer. "This thing came off jest the way it was planned. I'll make an arrest one of these days; this thing is goin' to be cleared up before I quit."

"I should think so," Eph remarked dryly. "Fifteen hundred bein' offered, I hear."

"Fifteen hundred," Dufors assured him, his mouth stuffed with food. "Better give me another handful of crackers, Eph. Only three parties could have done the job. It's bound to turn out to be one of 'em."

"Three, eh? Reckon yo're includin' Webb and his boy."

Dufors nodded. "It wasn't them; I'm dead certain of that!" He didn't say what made him so positive. Adkins stabbed him with a darting glance.

"Two from three leaves only him, eh?"

"It does, accordin' to my figgerin'." Dufors wiped his mouth with the back of his hand. "How much do I owe you for everythin', Eph?"

"Oh, two-bits is enough."

Dufors handed him a dollar and Adkins pulled out his purse to make change.

"Here you are, Frank. By the way, did you ever see one of these things?"

"Why, it's a fifty-cent piece," Dufors observed, taking the coin in his fingers. "Somebody's punched a couple holes in it. What's so out of the ordinary about it?"

"Why, that's one of them Columbian half dollars the Gov'ment minted specially for the Chicago World's Fair. A couple years ago there was a saloon down in Kingman that had some set right in the top of the bar till the boys started diggin' 'em out with their knives and walkin' off with 'em. Roberts dropped this one in the store yesterday. He's got four or five chained together for a watch fob. Reckon one came off when he was leanin' over the counter. I'm savin' it for him."

Dufors's obsidian eyes were suddenly as beady and bright as polished shoe buttons. He had racked his brain in a quest for something that he could use against Clay but in the wildest flights of fancy he had never conjured up anything to compare with this.

He turned the coin over in his palm and gazed at it with a brooding fascination. "Does anybody know you got this, Eph?" he got out tensely.

"No; I didn't find it till I swept up a little this mornin'." Old Eph cocked a puzzled eye at Dufors. "Hellsfire, Frank, there's no reason to take on about it; it ain't worth more'n a couple dollars."

"Eph, yo're crazy! Do you know what this thing is worth to you and me? Fifteen hundred dollars!"

The White Pine storekeeper blinked his eyes as understanding whipped through him.

"Half of that is seven-fifty, Eph. It's a nice little piece of money."

Adkins jerked his head affirmatively. "I could use it," he admitted, with a stony rasp. "But you git me straight, Frank; I ain' takin' no chances!"

"Chances?" Dufors jeered. "All I want you to do is forgit you ever saw this coin. I'll take care of everythin' else!"

They made their unholy bargain, without a twinge of conscience. Dufors was now anxious to get away from White Pine before anyone saw him there.

"Heck Barry is on his way up from Kingman," he told Eph, as he was leaving. Though he owed his official position to Sheriff Barry, he secretly despised the little man. "The county prosecutor's comin' along with him. I don't know whether they'll take Jennings back with them or bring him to trial in Mescal. It don't mean a damned thing to me now."

"Is Steve in any shape to go to trial?"

"Yeh, he's perkin' up considerable. Heck ain't foolin' me; I know why he's comin' to Mescal. It ain't on account of Steve Jennings. He's out to git my hide 'cause nothin's been done about the killing of the kid." Dufors laughed evilly. "I'll be ready for him, Eph!"

To return to the knoll east of the schoolhouse and conceal the half dollar in the dust, where he could find it at will, called for no great effort. When Barry, making the long trip around by Lund, got off the stage the next morning Dufors was, as he had predicted, ready for him.

In his younger days, Heck Barry had been a capable and honest officer. He was still as honest as politics would permit and considerably wiser.

"We got to break this case somehow," he said flatly, after hearing all Dufors had to say. "Papers all over the State hollering their heads off about it! Young boy murdered, and nothing being done! That's bad in an election year, especially when it comes on top of our being made to look silly by having a stockman's association bring in a big-time rustler like Steve Jennings and handing him over to us. You didn't find the empty cartridge or nothing, eh?"

"Not a thing," Dufors answered. "The killer picked up the ca'tridge, I figger. He wasn't no greenhorn, to think of that."

"Nine times out of ten that'd be true," Barry conceded. "We better go out there and have another look."

They were on Willow Creek by late afternoon. Dufors pointed out the spot from which the shot that killed Jeb had been fired. Barry got down on hands and knees and examined the ground carefully. When he neared the spot where the killer had lain, and where the half dollar was hidden, Dufors got down with him. Brushing the sand aside, he uncovered the coin. He called Heck and permitted him to pick it up.

"Well!" the little man exclaimed triumphantly. "Now we're getting somewheres! A Columbian half dollar! There ain't so many of them around. The way this one's been pierced, looks like it was being worn for an ornament."

"This nails it down, Heck!" Dufors cried, with pretended surprise and excitement. "Clay Roberts wears a watch fob made of half dollars like this! This one must have pulled off when he was stretched out here; he could have scuffed his boot and covered it up without ever knowin' it!"

"If the holes in this coin fit the links on the ones he's wearing, it's sure-fire!" the sheriff declared soberly. "Where is Roberts?"

"At Ringe's ranch on the Santa Bonita. At least, that's where he's stayin'."

"Okay! If he ain't there, we'll wait for him!"

Big John was seated on the gallery, when they rode in. Clay had been down in the basin in the afternoon and was having supper with the crew. He had seen Eudora. To find that she had taken the step he had so long advised was a welcome surprise, and he had returned to the Santa Bonita with a relieved mind.

Ringe called him to the door.

"I don't know what this means, Clay, but Sheriff Barry is here. He's got Dufors with him. They want to see you."

Clay took it calmly. "Whatever they've got to say, let's hear it," he said, following Ringe to the office.

Barry jerked a nod at him. Dufors looked on, wooden-faced.

"Roberts, does this Columbian half dollar belong to you?" the sheriff inquired, offering him the coin.

Clay looked at it carefully. "I imagine it does," was his answer. "It must have dropped off my fob. I missed it last night when I got back from the basin. I thought I'd lost it around the yard, or between here and White Pine. We looked for it this morning, and on the way up this evening, I stopped at White Pine and asked Adkins if he'd seen anything of it. Where did you find it?"

"Let's see if it fits," Barry said, ignoring the question. "Well, no question but it does!" He squared off and fixed Clay with a grim glance. "Roberts, are you familiar with the little rounded knoll, east of the Willow Creek schoolhouse, from which this Caney boy was killed?"

"I know where it is," Clay told him. "I've never had occasion to climb it since I've been here. Why do you ask?"

"That's where we found your coin, little better than an hour ago."

Ringe, seldom a profane man, ripped out a violent oath. "Barry, if that's where you found it, somebody planted it there!" he roared. He glared at Dufors with blazing eyes. "I recognize your hand in this, Dufors! I can smell a skunk a long ways!"

"Take it easy, John," Clay advised. "I don't know how this frame-up was worked but it won't help us any to lose our heads over it."

Heck gave him an approving nod. "That's the sensible way to look at it. You'll get a square deal from me. If you can knock out this evidence, you'll have plenty chance. I'll have to take you in, of course. You got a gun on you?"

"On my hip."

Dufors took possession of the gun.

"Heck Barry, I've known you for twenty years!" Ringe burst out afresh, his usually ruddy face purple with rage. "Before politics went to your head, you were on the up and up! You've got the wolves yapping at your heels now, and all you're interested in is making an arrest. I'm telling you to your teeth that I'm not convinced Roberts will get a square deal from you!"

The charge hit the nail on the head so squarely that it shook Hector Barry. "I ain't interested in the name-calling, John," he snapped.

"You will be before this is over!" Big John shot back. "You'll never railroad this boy to prison or worse as long as I can draw breath! The real taxpayers in this end of the county have been asking you for years to get rid of Dufors; and we gave you good and sufficient reasons! But you've strung along with him, thinking that was the way to get votes! Well, things have changed around here, Barry, and what you're up to now will settle your hash for keeps!"

Ranch hospitality required him to ask the sheriff and his deputy in to supper; but the invitation was not forthcoming for the first time in his long ownership of the Diamond R.

"You go along with them, Clay, and keep your chin up; I'll get the best lawyer money can buy, even if I have to go all the way to Tucson or Phoenix for him. You tell me what you want me to bring in to you tomorrow, and I'll fetch it."

Clay asked for the privilege of speaking to him privately for a minute. Barry granted it and stepped out on the gallery with Dufors.

"Eudora's got to be told, John," Clay said, his mouth tight. "I'd rather she heard it from you than anyone else."

"I'll see her sometime tomorrow. She'll take it pretty hard, I reckon. Maybe I better wait till I see what can be done in Mescal. Sam Bascom isn't much of a lawyer, but he'll have to do until I can send for a good man. Maybe Bascom can get you released on a writ or something. They'll have to give you a hearing before they can bind you over to stand trial. I'll be there with Bascom; if the coin is the only evidence they have against you, they may not vote an indictment. There's just a chance, Clay, that I might be able to bring Miss Stoddard some good news."

"All right, do as you think best. I don't want her dragged into this mess, John. I'm pretty sure she knows something about what happened that afternoon that she hasn't felt free to tell me. Don't urge her to talk; if she brings it up, that'll be different. But unless it's really important, don't let her do anything about it."

Ringe nodded. "You can trust me to use my judgment."

When they finished talking and stepped out on the gallery, they found most of the Diamond R crew gathered there, their faces rocky with concern for Clay. Several, including Cleve Johnson, slapped him on the back encouragingly and assured him of their support.

More than once on the long ride to Mescal, Clay recalled his remark to Eudora that he knew of nothing Frank Dufors wouldn't do for $1,500. This was proof of it.

It'll just about kill her when she learns it's her bracelet they're using to pin this thing on me! he thought, biting back a groan.

Dawn was breaking by the time they reached Mescal. Dufors shoved Clay into a cell.

"That'll cool you off," he muttered, walking away.

In the next cell, Steve Jennings rose up on his bunk as he heard the steel door clang and blinked owlishly at his next-door neighbor. His sleepy eyes widened incredulously as he recognized Clay.

"You in the jug, too?" he growled. "What for?"

"They say I killed that Caney boy."

"What!" Steve yelped. "That's the craziest thing I ever heard! You were up in the box

218

canyon with me and the boys that afternoon and night! I'll tell these stinkin' coyotes where they git off!"

Clay shook his head. "You remember saying to me, Steve, that it was strange, my being there, doing what I could for you? I told you no one would understand it. That still goes; if you try to come through for me it'll put me deeper in the hole than ever."

Jennings bristled angrily. "You mean my word ain't good enough?"

"Your word is good enough for me, but the State won't take it. You'll very likely be in the pen by the time I come to trial. If my lawyer put you on the stand, the prosecution would tear you to pieces, and the cry would go up that if I had to fall back on a convicted rustler to pull my chestnuts out of the fire that I was guilty on the face of it."

Clay explained what the evidence was against him.

"You can see what they'd do to anything you had to say, Steve. Why was I up there with you? What was the proposition I made? It would all come out, and the jury would laugh in your face."

"I reckon they would," Steve admitted with a savage snarl. "But don't put me in the pen yet, Clay; I ain't stickin' around here much longer." He lowered his voice cautiously. "I'm keepin' in touch with Slick and Utah; they ain't far away. They can damn near sneeze hard enough to blow down this calaboose—if they can't think up somethin' easier. When I go, you better walk out with me!"

"It wouldn't do me any good to bust out and have this thing hanging over my head. It'd mean living outside the law."

"Hunh!" Jennings snorted contemptuously. "It'd mean livin'—period! Better men than you have been railroaded on less than Dufors has got! Just how do you figure you're goin' to beat this case? You ain't got no witnesses, no alibi, nothin'!"

"I don't know just yet what I'm going to do," Clay confessed. "They'll yank me up for a hearing sometime today, I suppose. I'll have to figure out something."

"Give it a whirl," Steve muttered. "Mebbe it'll help you to make up your mind. You don't want to take too long about it; there may be somethin' stirrin' tonight."

Clay gazed at him soberly. "As soon as that, eh?"

Steve nodded. "I'll know for certain when Singer brings in my breakfast."

Chapter Seventeen

The Jail Buster

News of Clay's arrest did not spread over the basin until late in the day. As a consequence, the children were not in position to do any tattling. With that source of information failing her, Eudora went through the morning blissfully unaware of what had happened.

Harvey Hume was equally uninformed, even at noon, when he came in from the creek, where he was cutting poles for a new corral. He returned to the creek after dinner, and it was almost two o'clock, when Virgil came charging up on his big bay horse to tell him Clay was in jail.

Harvey's first thought was of Eudora. "I hate to ride over there, looking like this," he said, "but I better do it. I'll douse my head in the creek and clean up a little and get going, if you'll loan me your horse."

When he reached the schoolhouse, he called Eudora outside. His excitement filled her with alarm before he said a word.

"It's Clay!" she cried, her cheeks draining

white. "Something terrible has happened to him!"

Harvey nodded gravely. "Barry and Dufors arrested him last night at the Santa Bonita."

Her knees suddenly felt so weak she had to brace herself to hear the rest of it. In a daze, she dismissed school. Getting up behind Harvey, she rode home with him at once. Virgil had returned to the house and repeated his story to Harvey's mother. She ran out and helped Eudora down.

Eudora threw her arms about her and did not try to check her tears for a minute.

"You cry as much as you like, child; it will relieve you, and then you can get a grip on yourself," Mrs. Hume told her. "We all know he's innocent."

"I don't know what to do, Martha! It would be foolish for me to see that man Dufors! And to think it had to be that silly bracelet of mine that led to this! It makes me feel responsible! I never should have given it to Clay; I should have known it was so flimsy it would come apart!"

Only the previous evening, she had told Mrs. Hume that she and Clay were to be married as soon as school closed.

"I know how much you love him, Eudora; that's why you feel you are to blame. But you mustn't; it was not your fault. It could have

222

been his pocketknife, or anything else he might have dropped. Come over to the bench and sit down with me. I'm sure they'll have to turn Mr. Roberts free. He'll be all right, you wait and see."

The expression she caught on Harvey's and Virgil's faces said they did not share her optimism. She gave them a warning glance.

"If you think you'd like to go to town, I'll hitch the team," Harvey offered. "It might comfort you to be with your aunt and uncle."

"It isn't comforting I want, Harvey," Eudora declared tremulously. "I want to do something to help Clay!"

For whatever it was worth, she wanted to come forward with Verne's confession. But to whom was she to speak? She thought of John Ringe, Clay's friend. He was like a rock—strong and reliable, Clay had said. Yes, she decided, she would go to John Ringe!

"I'll be glad to take you up," Harvey assured her.

"There's one thing about John Ringe," Virgil spoke up. "He sticks with his friends. He'll see this thing through for Clay, Miss Stoddard. And he ain't the only friend Clay's got!"

"You hitch the team, Virgil, while I run a razor over my face and get into a clean shirt," said Harvey. "I'm anxious to hear what Mr. Ringe has got to say too."

When they reached the Santa Bonita, Hod Willoughby, the Diamond R straw boss, when Big John was away from the ranch, told them the boss wasn't there.

"He said he'd be back this evenin', folks. If you care to wait, you can make yoreselves comfortable on the gallery. You'll find some chairs. Usually a little breeze playin' along there this time o' day."

"We'll wait," Eudora told him. "And thanks for being so kind."

Hod hung on, hunting for words. Finally, he said, "Any news from town about Clay, ma'am? It's hit us purty hard here."

With a glance, Eudora urged Harvey to answer for her.

"The report we got was brought out from Mescal by Jim Tulliver," Harvey said. "He left town early, so we don't know what's happened there during the day."

Hod wagged his head regretfully. "The old man'll have somethin' to tell us when he gits here," he muttered, turning away.

Eudora settled down to wait with Harvey. She refused to speculate on what might have occurred in Mescal, even when he suggested the news from town might be good. She felt he was only saying it to buck her up. She told herself over and over that it had been unforgivable folly to protect Verne; that she should have told Clay at once of the boy's admissions. It became like the dismal tolling of a bell at sea in her mind.

The crew began to gather at the far end of the gallery, waiting for supper. Soon after they filed in, Hod appeared again.

"Supper's on the table, folks," he said. "Will you come in?"

"I couldn't eat a bite," Eudora answered. "You have supper, Harvey."

"The boss often has his meals in the office, Miz Stoddard," said Hod. "I can have somethin' brought in if you don't feel like settin' down with a bunch of men."

"Thanks so much, Mr. Willoughby, but I'll just wait here."

Hod nodded, impressed; he was seldom addressed as Mr. Willoughby. Harvey followed him to the dining-room.

The twilight had faded into black night before Big John arrived. He had stopped at Harvey's place and been told Eudora had gone to the Santa Bonita.

He got down from his horse heavily. Things had not gone his way but he knew he had to put on a brave face to her.

She got up to meet him. He put a fatherly arm about her shoulders and led her back to her chair and sat down beside her. He had a word of greeting for Harvey.

225

"I stopped at your place on the way up. Your mother told me you were here." He took out an enormous handkerchief and mopped his face. "Been a trying day. I thought we might be able to knock this thing out before it went any further. We weren't able to do it."

"Please be frank with me, Mr. Ringe," Eudora pleaded, her eyes searching his face.

"I'm going to be," the big man assured her. "I'm not going to give you any nonsense about this not being serious. Clay's been bound over to await trial. Bert Caulkins, the county prosecutor, is in Mescal; he argued at the hearing that their evidence was enough to justify an indictment."

Eudora sat frozen in her chair. Big John's sympathy ran out to her. He pressed her hand.

"Don't take it so hard, little girl," he urged. "We've just begun to fight, I promise you! This whole framed-up case against Clay can be knocked into a cocked hat if we can find out how that coin came into Dufors's possession. Clay doesn't know where it was lost. He thinks it might have been here." The big man shook his head at the thought. "I just can't believe I've got anyone working for me who'd be skunk enough to sell him out for part of the reward money!"

He went on to explain in detail just what had taken place in town. There really wasn't much to tell. Barry and Dufors had sworn they had found the half dollar on the knoll; Clay had admitted ownership of it. That had been enough.

"Wasn't it brought out that Clay discovered that very afternoon where the Jennings gang was hiding?" Eudora asked, trying to steady her voice. "You know he was able to lead you to their hideout because of what he learned. Doesn't that prove he was far away from Willow Creek? Jennings is in jail. Can't he be made to talk?"

"Clay and I discussed it and decided it wouldn't help him to try to build up that sort of an alibi. There must be something better; we've got to start digging it up. If anybody knows anything that'll help him, I don't believe they'll hesitate to speak."

It was not a too guileless invitation for her to tell him what she knew. He wasn't forgetting his promise to Clay. On the other hand, he didn't propose to leave any stone unturned.

Eudora needed no further urging; she was anxious, even determined, to tell all she knew. With Harvey and Ringe sitting on the edge of their chairs, she acquainted them with the circumstances that had led up to Verne's confession, and, without missing a word, she repeated what the boy had said.

"You never should have held this back, Miss Stoddard! It would have been worth twice as

227

much to Clay if it had come out before he was arrested!" Ringe's great voice rumbled with intense feeling. "I know what was in your mind; but trying to spare that Nichols boy his just deserts for what he'd done was a mistake! When he's put on the stand now, he'll deny he ever made a confession to you!"

"He's already attempted to do that," Eudora confessed. "Mr. Ringe—will the fact that I have given Clay my promise to marry him, weaken what I have to say so much that it can be thrown out?"

"Well, it can't be thrown out!" the big man declared vehemently. "But there's no question but what your being engaged will cast some doubt on your testimony. Bert Caulkins has a bitter tongue; he'll shame and discredit you if he can."

"Let him do his worst!" Eudora said defiantly. "He can tear me to pieces, but he'll never make me change a word of what I've just told you and Harvey!"

"Clay has to be considered," Ringe said heavily. "He told me a dozen times that he didn't want you dragged into this case. He didn't know, of course, that you had anything like this to say. It's so important that I don't see how he can afford to say no to you."

"If I can talk with him, Mr. Ringe, I'm sure I can win him over!" Eudora's eyes blurred and she turned her face away. "I've got to see him!"

"You better stay here tonight," the big man advised. "We'll start for town about four in the morning. We'll have a chance to talk everything over while we're driving in. I don't want you to worry about the school. Tomorrow's Saturday; if you don't feel you can go on, come Monday, we'll just cut the term short and close the school."

"I'll be able to continue," Eudora insisted. "I made myself that promise and I'll keep it."

Hod was hovering in the background. He got Big John's attention. "Elmer's holdin' supper for you, boss. The boys have been done some time."

"All right, Hod; you have Elmer put whatever he's got on the table. I'll be in directly. Harvey, have you and Miss Stoddard had anything to eat?"

"I went in some time ago, Mr. Ringe," Harvey said. "Miss Stoddard didn't feel she could eat anything."

"Well, a little supper won't hurt you, my dear," the big man declared. He took Eudora's arm and she let him persuade her to have a bite.

"I'll be going home, I guess," Harvey told them. "I'd appreciate it if you'd stop in tomorrow evening on your way back, Mr. Ringe. It doesn't matter how late it happens to be."

Big John nodded. "I'll do it," he promised.

After supper, he showed Eudora to the room she was to use. It was airy and comfortable.

"I hope you'll be able to get some sleep," he said. "You don't want to get to town all worn out. My room is down the hall. If you need me for anything, just rap. You may have to bang pretty loud; I'm a sound sleeper."

The house grew quiet presently. Eudora undressed, but she found sleep impossible. She carried a chair to the open window and sat there for hours, a blanket around her shoulders, for the night was cool.

She didn't know how late it was, when she heard someone ride into the yard. She thought it must be three or later. In a few minutes, footsteps sounded on the stairs. Whoever it was, went to Big John's room. The blurred murmur of voices followed.

Eudora thought it might be something in connection with the ranch, but Ringe came down the hall with the man who had awakened him. He rapped on her door.

"You better get dressed, Miss Stoddard, and come down as soon as you can," he called. "Someone here to see you."

That it must be some messenger her uncle had sent out from town seemed the most logical explanation; it could hardly be anyone from out in the basin. She dressed hurriedly. When she got down, she found a light burning in the office.

"Clay!" she cried, on reaching the door. "It's you!"

She ran to him and threw her arms about him wildly.

"Oh, darling, I'm so happy!" she sobbed. "I knew they'd have to release you!"

"That's not quite the way it was," Clay said, holding her close. "They didn't let me out, Eudora; I busted jail. At least. I walked out."

Eudora looked up at him in stunned dismay. "Oh, no!" she cried. "They'll hold this against you, too! They'll say it's further proof of your guilt!"

"They will if they catch me; I don't aim to be caught." She had never heard him speak so soberly. "I knew this thing was coming. Steve told me a few minutes after I was locked up. I wasn't interested at first, but the way things went yesterday changed my mind. I could see that Barry and this district attorney had decided to go all the way with Dufors and grease the skids for me."

"But Clay, Verne Nichols confessed to me the day after the shooting that he killed Jeb! Mr. Ringe was taking me to town in the morning so I could make a statement—"

"I know, Eudora; John just told me all about it. I don't think it would have saved me. Anyhow, I wouldn't see you dragged through the mire to save my hide. This way, I've got a chance to prove my innocence. It may take a long time, but I'll do it!"

"Did Jennings's pardners do any shooting when they cracked the jail?" Ringe asked.

"No, Carroll and Utah Sims had Dufors covered before he knew what was happening. They stuck a gag in his mouth and locked him up in one of the cells. Dufors's horse was outside at the rail; it wasn't later than nine o'clock. I took the horse."

"They'll find Dufors in a few hours, Clay. They'll be after you."

"I know it, John; I can't stay here very long."

"Clay, I can't let you go! I can't!" Eudora cried, clinging to him frantically.

His face whipped hard and flat suddenly. Unlacing her fingers, he held her off at arm's length. "Eudora—with this trouble hanging over me, do you love me enough to leave Arizona with me tonight? I know I shouldn't ask it. But I need you too! We can't go by stage; they'll be looking for me there. The trail over Ute Pass will get us into Utah. We can find someone to marry us. Until things quiet down, we can go to Nevada and live at the mine. This is for better or for worse, and it's forever, my dearest!"

"My answer is yes—no matter what it costs!" Eudora's voice broke. Clay took her into his arms tenderly.

"You're all that matters to me, Clay! But there's my aunt and uncle. They're old. To go without a word will crush them, darling!"

"I'll see them and explain why it had to be this way," Ringe offered. "It isn't as though you weren't coming back, little girl. I promise the two of you that I'll be busy while you're away. This rotten deal cries out to heaven for justice, and I'll get it for you. I don't want you to write me, Clay; Dufors will be watching the post office for some word to come from you. When I have something to tell you, I'll come to you. I won't risk putting anything in writing. Nevada is a long way off. Barring accident, you'll be safe out there."

Clay told him where he and Eudora could be found.

"Don't get impatient if the months go by without your seeing anything of me," the big man cautioned. "I'll be trying every day." He walked over to the safe. "I'll get your money; you'll need it."

Clay ran up to his room and stuffed a few things in a saddlebag and got his rifle. He found Ringe and Eudora waiting for him at the foot of the stairs.

"I don't want to hurry you," the old cowman said, "but an hour saved now may come in handy. I'll go down the yard with you and get some horses."

Eudora turned to him just before Clay helped her into the saddle. "What a good friend you are!" she murmured, pressing her cheek against his. "When you see Aunt Jude, tell her not to grieve for me; I know I'm doing the right thing. I'm not afraid."

"There's no reason why you should be," Ringe returned, his voice heavy with emotion. "This boy will never let you down, Eudora. If I'd ever had a son of my own, I couldn't have wished for him to turn out any better." He glanced at Clay. "We'll just say so long for the present. I'll stand here till you're across the creek."

Clay nodded. "So long, John," he said, tight of lip.

Big John turned back to the house, when they had faded into the night. "They're a fine pair!" he muttered grimly. "With God's help, I'll put up a fight for them!"

Chapter Eighteen

Good News

Summer passed and the crystal-clear days of fall followed. One morning, from the doorway of the cabin, high on the shoulder of Buckskin Mountain, Clay looked to the west and found the tip of Disaster Peak white with snow. It reminded him that weeks and months had been slipping by. No word had come from John Ringe.

Clay had hired an experienced hardrock miner to work with him. They had exposed a small vein of gold-bearing quartz. It assayed high, but how rich the mine was remained to be determined. News of the find leaked down over the Hinkey Summit to the little town of Paradise Valley. On one of his weekly trips below, for supplies, Clay had been offered three times what he had paid for the property.

Until now, no whisper of what had happened in Mescal had caught up with him. It failed to ease his mind, for, from his own experience as a detective, he knew that the passing of time held only a false security for a wanted man. Winnemucca, the county seat, with its railroad, lay 40-odd miles to the south. Though he arranged his business so that he had no occasion for going there, he realized if word of him got that far that the sheriff of Humboldt County would find him promptly.

"I found a little house in Paradise today that we can rent for the winter," he told Eudora, at the end of the week. "We'll be all right up here until the first of November."

"Will you be safe there, Clay?"

"As safe as I am here. I thought we'd be seeing something of John before this. It's roundup time now; it'll keep him tied down for a couple weeks. We'll just have to wait." He saw Eudora wince.

"Oh, I know how hard it is on you!" he exclaimed, taking her into his arms. "You've never complained, but I can see it's wearing you down."

"I'm not thinking of myself, Clay. Despite everything, I've been happy here. So happy, darling! Honestly, I have!"

"Do you want me to write John?"

"No, we'll wait. He warned you not to write. My faith in him is as strong as ever. I don't believe a roundup, or anything else, would hold him back if he had good news for us."

The haze of Indian summer crept into the sky. But for the shadow hanging over them, life on Buckskin would have been a pure delight. They could see the road that led up to the big

National mine. Teams and horsemen often moved over it, but they came no further and it was seldom, indeed, that anyone toiled up the road Clay had cut. One noon, in mid-October, however, a buckboard slowly negotiated the steep climb.

"Clay, do you suppose it's the sheriff?" Eudora queried breathlessly, as she got up from the table and ran to the door.

He studied their visitor with narrowed eyes. Suddenly, recognition electrified him.

"Dora, it's Ringe! Look at the size of him! It's Big John!" Catching her hand, they ran down the road together. The big man waved to them.

"Good grief!" he boomed. "Talk about Arizona roads! They're boulevards compared to what you've got here!"

He climbed down from the buckboard and embraced the two of them. "I've got good news for you! I hardly know where to begin."

"Has Clay been cleared?" Eudora demanded, unable to control her voice. "That's the important thing, Mr. Ringe!"

"Honey, I wouldn't be here if he hadn't! But that takes the punch out of my story. There was a mix-up about the reward money, Clay. Even though you got away, it was paid. Dufors tried to renege on the deal he'd made and keep it all. Eph Adkins was in it with him; he found that half dollar in the store. You can imagine the noise he made when he saw himself being done out of his half. It brought Barry up to Mescal. And humble the little runt was; he'd changed his tune considerable. He was all for arresting Eph for bearing false witness and so forth; I thought it'd be better not to bring any charges if Eph would talk. Barry agreed to it, and we got the whole story. Dufors was the rat I wanted to get!"

"Looks like you had him dead to rights," Clay said.

"We sure did! But Dufors was hard to find; he'd lit out for Mexico."

"Does that mean there isn't a warrant out on me?"

"How could there be in the face of what I've just told you? And that isn't half of it. We've got a new deputy sheriff in Mescal. I had something to do with getting him appointed. He's Virgil Hume."

"Virgil?" Clay echoed. "He ought to be a fine man for the job."

"He's done all right so far. The two of us got our heads together over what Verne Nichols told you, Eudora. We put it up to Webb. The upshot of it was that Webb surrendered the boy. On account of his youth he's been sent down the State to the Industrial School. They'll keep him there five or six years."

Clay and Eudora couldn't have asked for

more. The weeks and months of waiting, of anxiety and uncertainty were gone forever now.

"I saw the Stoddards just before I left," the big man told Eudora. "They're fine, and just waiting for you to come back—you will go back with me, won't you?" He was speaking to the two of them.

"We'll go back for a visit, John," Clay answered. "We've still got a little traveling to do in Texas too. But the mine's looking so good I've got to stick with it."

"Good Lord!" Ringe boomed. "Do you mean to tell me that after spending your life with cows and cowmen you're going to be satisfied to settle down here and burrow in the ground like a confounded gopher?"

"There may be a pot of gold in this hole, John," Clay said laughingly. "That makes quite a difference."

"Well, we'll see!" Big John snorted. "You'll have to spend the winter somewhere. You can do it in Mescal as well as anywhere else. I'm telling you the Diamond R is pretty big and lonely without you fussing around. I may have a proposition to make you before spring comes up again." He tightened his arm around Eudora and grinned at her. "It'll come out all right if the two of us work together on him."

Books are produced in the United States using U.S.-based materials

Books are printed using a revolutionary new process called THINKtech™ that lowers energy usage by 70% and increases overall quality

Books are durable and flexible because of smythe-sewing

Paper is sourced using environmentally responsible foresting methods and the paper is acid-free

Center Point Large Print
600 Brooks Road / PO Box 1
Thorndike, ME 04986-0001 USA

(207) 568-3717

US & Canada:
1 800 929-9108
www.centerpointlargeprint.com